KEEP YOUR FRIENDS CLOSE

JOANNE RYAN

Boldwood

First published in Great Britain in 2024 by Boldwood Books Ltd.

Copyright © Joanna Ryan, 2024

Cover Design by 12 Orchards Ltd.

Cover Photography: Shutterstock

A CIP catalogue record for this book is available from the British Library.

Paperback ISBN 978-1-83533-702-8

Large Print ISBN 978-1-83533-698-4

Hardback ISBN 978-1-83533-697-7

Ebook ISBN 978-1-83533-695-3

Kindle ISBN 978-1-83533-696-0

Audio CD ISBN 978-1-83533-703-5

MP3 CD ISBN 978-1-83533-700-4

Digital audio download ISBN

Boldwood Books Ltd
23 Bowerdean Street
London SW6 3TN
www.boldwoodbooks.com

For Pete, with love.

PROLOGUE

It's the black, unruly curls that first catch my eye. I stop and watch as he weaves his way through the throng of people.

Marco.

He has the same tall, muscular body, but more than that, it's the walk: the confident stride, the almost regal way he holds his head – as if he's the most important person in the world.

Which he was, for me, for a while.

But it can't be Marco; it's impossible.

Because he's dead.

I know he's dead because I killed him.

1

EIGHT MONTHS AGO

The explosion is so loud that it makes my ears ring.

I look around the apartment in confusion, expecting to see the windows blown out and debris everywhere, but there's nothing; the room looks exactly as it did when I arrived here. The same blond furniture and bland décor: beige and minimalist, a typical rental.

There's a weird smell in the air that makes me think of bonfire night, but I don't think it's fireworks. I look down at my hand and realise where the noise came from, but what I see doesn't make any sense because my brain is refusing to function. My head feels clouded and fuzzy, as if I have cotton wool in my ears.

Something has happened.

I've done something bad... very bad.

Marco was shouting at me. I remember that much. On and on and on and I push the memory of it away because the things he said hurt and I don't want to think about them.

He wouldn't stop, and I just wanted him to shut up.

Shut up.

He laughed at me and called me names. Vile names and insults that soon turned to pushing and shoving: the precursor to the violence that always followed. But it didn't come to that.

It stopped.

I stopped it.

I close down my mind and try to forget. I'm very good at forgetting. I can close my eyes and make it all go away, but there's something stopping me: something that I need to do.

Something important.

I look down at my hand and stare at my fingers and will them to move, and slowly they begin to unfurl and release the handle of the gun. I watch as it drops to the floor, where it lands with a muffled thud on the carpet.

I look at it lying there and try to remember where it came from.

'Mia! Mia!'

I hear Carrie's voice over the humming in my ears and I look up to see her standing in the doorway, staring at me. I close my eyes and try to concentrate on the important thing that I have to do.

'Mia!'

She sounds so far away, but when I open my eyes again, she's standing right in front of me. Where did she come from? For a moment, I wonder if I'm asleep and this is one of my nightmares. I have them sometimes when I'm feeling anxious or stressed. There's music playing, but it sounds distant and I can't hear it properly, but the song is familiar, something about hot dogs and jumping frogs. A memory pushes its way through the fog in my brain, but disappears before I can grasp hold of it.

But I remember enough to know that I've always hated that song.

'Mia, what have you done?' Carrie sounds panic-stricken; she has that shrill edge to her voice that people get when they're on the verge of losing it. I've not heard her like that before; she's always so calm and sensible. My rock.

But now she sounds a lot like Gramma used to.

'MIA! WHAT HAVE YOU DONE?' Carrie's face is so close to mine, I can feel her breath and I think she might have spat in my face. I know she didn't mean to. Her eyes are wide and her mouth has gone all slack like a rubber band, as if she doesn't know whether to laugh or cry.

'I'm not sure,' I manage to say. 'Something bad. I think.' I'm having difficulty forming the words and they come out slowly. My mouth feels as if it's full of something. Cotton wool: it's spread from my brain to my mouth. The thought of it makes me feel sick and I retch, tasting red wine.

'Oh my God, Mia. He's dead.'

Carrie's no longer in front of me. Now she's on the other side of the room and she's kneeling down, leaning over something.

Someone.

Marco.

After a while, she looks up at me and slowly shakes her head. I want to tell her to leave him, that I need her more than he does, but my mouth has stopped working again. She should be with me. *Come to me, Carrie, come and help me,* I implore silently. *Put me first, like you always do.*

She starts to cry with loud sobs that echo around the room, and I want her to stop. She's mumbling 'Jesus', repeatedly. I want to tell her He can't help her, but it's too much effort to even try to form the words.

A memory of Gramma swims into my head. *You'll go too far one day, Mia, and then what will you do?* She used to say it to me all the time.

What if today is that day? I think it is.

Carrie's here; I feel the warmth of her arms around me and I'm so relieved. I melt into her and know that everything is going to be okay. She shouldn't have left me on my own; Carrie's been my best friend forever and she always looks after me. She's whispering that we have to go and she's trying to lead me towards the door. I don't know why she's whispering because there's no one else around to hear her. My legs feel wobbly and I don't know if I can move them. I try to wrap my arms around Carrie to cling onto her, but my arms flap around uselessly like a seal's flippers, unwilling to do as they're bid. It's as if they're made of jelly.

Jelly arms and legs. A laugh bubbles up inside me because it's funny, so funny. Or maybe I'm hysterical.

I think I'm hysterical.

We stop after only a few wobbly steps and Carrie lowers me down onto the sofa and the relief at no longer having to stand up is immense. I flop backwards and close my eyes and feel the cushion shift as Carrie sits down next to me.

'We'll rest for a moment. Let you get over the shock.'

We sit silently for minutes, or maybe it's hours.

'What happened, Mia?' Carrie says. 'Can you tell me what happened? Where did the gun come from?'

I open my eyes and stare at her. The light is fading now, the night drawing in so rapidly, but it's too early, much too early for it to be dark.

I want to go to sleep.

I need to go to sleep.

'It's going to be all right, Mia,' Carrie whispers. 'Everything's going to be all right. I'll make everything all right, I promise.'

I want so badly to believe her, but I know the truth; I know that this time, it's never going to be all right.

This time, I've gone too far.

2

NOW

'What do you think? Too much...?' I give a little twirl and watch Carrie's face.

'Stop fishing, you know you never look less than perfect. Unlike me.' Carrie pulls a face before peering into the mirror and applying a layer of lipstick.

'Now who's fishing?'

She laughs and I pick up my glass of Prosecco and finish the last mouthful. I know I look good. I'm not being disingenuous when I say that; just stating the facts. Strangely, whilst it's perfectly acceptable to brag about being clever, rich or successful, admitting to being beautiful is frowned upon and seen as conceit, even when it's just an accident of birth in the same way that being clever is.

I'm constantly judged on how I look by others, yet am supposed to pretend that I'm oblivious to my appearance. I'd be lying if I pretended not to know that I'm attractive but it's not as if I go around bragging about it. Some people – weirdly, mostly women – seem to actively dislike me because of my looks. They treat me as if I've done something wrong even though I haven't. I don't know what I'm supposed to do other than be nice to them to prove that good looks don't mean I'm a bad person. I can't exactly hide my face, can I? I suppose I could make myself look less attractive, but I don't think I should have to do that. No one expects clever people to make themselves look stupid, do they?

Carrie doesn't give a hoot about appearances and doesn't hold my looks against me. She's the least vain person in the world and barely notices what she's wearing. She has zero interest in fashion. She'd probably be wearing a tracksuit tonight if I hadn't forced her into wearing one of my dresses. She's so pretty when she makes an effort, but she's genuinely not bothered how she looks and is far more interested in having a successful career. We're so different in so many ways; maybe that's one of the reasons we've been the absolute best of friends forever. What could be better than having your best friend living with you in your apartment?

'Don't pre-game too much, Mia; it's an art exhibition we're going to, not a club,' Carrie says, frowning at the bottle in my hand.

'Okay, Mum.' I laugh and pour us both another glass to stop her from giving me a lecture or touching on the subject that we don't want to talk about. 'I need a few drinks to get through the tediousness of tonight. Thank God you're coming with me to relieve the dullness otherwise I'd have had to pretend to be ill or something. Anyway, it doesn't matter if I'm the tiniest bit tipsy because as I always say, Sebastian needs me to bring the party to the gallery otherwise everyone will die from boredom.'

Carrie can't hide the distasteful look that flashes across her face at the mention of Sebastian's name. I wish they liked each other more, but for some unfathomable reason, it was hate at first sight.

'You're sure he doesn't mind me coming?' she asks.

'Of course not!' I lie. 'The more the merrier. It's very important when an artist has their first exhibition to have as many people as possible attend. There's nothing worse than a half-empty gallery with tumbleweed blowing through.'

I put her glass of Prosecco on the dressing table in front of her.

'Hurry up and drink it because we don't want to be late.'

She picks up the glass and takes the tiniest sip possible before putting it down again. I'm hoping tonight will perk her up a bit; she's been very quiet these last few months. She's never been much of a party animal but recently she's turned into a stay-at-home hermit and she's only twenty-six. She rarely goes anywhere except to work, and that's not healthy. I feel guilty that I'm out and about enjoying myself most nights and she's alone in the apartment watching TV soaps or beavering away at the office.

But especially guilty considering what she's done for me.

I push the thought away and remind myself that we've made a pact to not talk or even think about it. That night's events feel rather unreal to me now because I've pushed it so far down that it almost feels like a dream. A very bad dream. A nightmare. Thinking of it like that is my way of coping with it and makes the horror of what I've done more bearable. Even now, although I know how it happened, I struggle to believe that I was so stupid. But as Carrie reminds me, there is nothing to be gained by rehashing it over and over again, because all it'll do is make me feel worse. The more we talk about it, the more I'll think about it and I need to forget.

What's done is done and cannot be undone.

Not that I know what's been done. I mean, obviously, I know what I did but after that, events are very vague. Vague as in – I have no idea what Carrie did to sort everything out. She says that it's better that I don't know because then I can't start imagining horrible things or, God forbid, telling people. Obviously, I'd never tell anyone; I couldn't, because it would be the end of me and of Carrie, too, and why should she suffer for something that she did for me? I know with absolute certainty that Carrie will never tell a living soul what we did; she's an absolute expert at keeping things to herself. She kept her real background secret for nearly a year when we were at school together. Even *I* never guessed.

I don't want the details of how she got rid of him, but that doesn't stop my mind from imaging all sorts. The nights are the worst; once I'm asleep, I have no control over my dreams and that's when it all comes out, like an action replay. Although the nightmares are becoming less frequent as the months go by, so I'm hoping with time that they'll stop completely.

Sometimes, I think maybe we should talk about it

because there are so many questions I want answers to and if I just knew a little bit, it might relieve my anxiety. But the trouble is, I know if I start asking questions, I won't be able to stop and I'll end up driving myself – and Carrie – mad.

'There. I'm ready.' Carrie picks up her glass, stares at it for a moment before putting it back down on the dressing table. She stands up. She's not much of a drinker.

'How do I look?' She walks over to stand in front of the full-length mirror and smooths down the skirt of the dark-blue dress with her hands.

'Beautiful,' I say, standing next to her and slipping my arm around her waist. 'That colour really suits you. You can keep it if you like; I don't really wear it.'

I've never worn it, actually; I bought it in the sales last year and it's been hanging in the wardrobe ever since. It's not really me; it looks much better on Carrie. She looks elegant and understated.

'I couldn't let you do that,' Carrie says, shaking her head. 'It's designer.'

I shrug. 'It's up to you. I was going to put it in the charity bag, anyway.' Immediately, I know that I've said the wrong thing; I should think before I open my big mouth. Carrie's a bit uptight about money; she's

big on not being wasteful and recycling and everything. She thinks buying expensive clothes is pointless when you can buy something more or less the
same for a fraction of the price. She has this thing
about money: about not having any. Well, she has
some now of course, because she has a good job and
is going places, but she doesn't come from money.
She's not used to spending it and thinks she has to
justify every purchase as 'worthwhile'. Like most
people who aren't used to having money, she gives it
far too much importance.

'How glamourous we look!' I point at our reflec-
tions in an attempt to gloss over my gaff. 'Everyone
will be so busy ogling us that poor old Tally won't get
a look in selling her godawful pictures.'

'Mia! That's a bit harsh.'

'Just telling it how it is. I have to lie through my
teeth to *her* face but I can be totally honest with you.
Her paintings are ghastly; all female angst and
misery and great gobs of black oil paint splattered all
over the place. It's enough to send anybody into a
deep depression. God knows why anyone would
want any of them hanging on their walls; I wouldn't.'

'Sebastian won't be pleased if no one buys any of
them, will he?'

'Oh, he needn't worry, they'll sell like hot cakes,

because the people coming tonight have far too much money and very little taste.' I might not like Tally's style, but I have a knack for knowing what people want and what sells. I've surprised Sebastian with my 'commercial eye', as he calls it, because it's not what he employed me for. 'Come on, we'd better get a move on or else we'll be late.'

I let go of Carrie and pick up my handbag and chiffon wrap from the dresser.

'You're sure this isn't too short and showing too much leg?' She turns this way and that in the mirror, taking one more look at herself.

'It's perfect and your legs look as if they go on forever. Now come on, the cab will be here any minute and you know they don't bother waiting around.'

We let ourselves out of the apartment and head down the corridor, straight into the lift, and descend the three floors to the foyer. The lift doors have barely opened before Owen, the on-shift security guard, bobs out from behind his desk.

'Your taxi's waiting outside. He was all ready to drive off when you weren't here, but I persuaded him to hang on for five minutes.'

'You're such a sweetheart, Owen, that's so nice of you. What would we do without you?' I flash him a smile and he bounds over to the entrance and presses the button to release the doors that lead to the street. We hurry through and out into the waiting cab.

'Art gallery you're going to, innit?' The cab driver glances over his shoulder at us as we climb into the back, a miserable expression on his face.

I open my mouth to reply but the car jolts and we pull out into the London traffic, barely giving us time to close the doors.

'I've got the address,' he bellows, without turning round.

'In a hurry, isn't he?' I mutter as I attempt to plug my seatbelt in.

'I'll say. Lucky that Owen got him to wait.'

'We could have walked because it's not far, but I didn't fancy it in these heels.' I look down at my towering, strappy shoes.

'He's definitely got a crush on you,' Carrie says.

'Who, the cab driver?' I giggle.

'Owen. He can't get out from behind that desk quick enough once he sees you. He's like an over-excited puppy; his tongue was practically hanging out of his mouth when you spoke to him.'

'Maybe it's you he has the crush on.'

Carrie snorts. 'No. As if. Ever since he took over from the last guy, he's always hovering around, waiting to catch a glimpse of you.'

Of course I've noticed. Owen is very good looking and hard to miss: thick, black, curly hair, olive skin, well-muscled and well over six foot. He has just the sort of looks I go for.

He actually looks quite a bit like Marco did.

But there the similarity ends; there is no air of danger about Owen, no brooding intensity or simmering anger. Owen is keen and eager to please and therefore not in the least bit attractive to me.

'Hmm. He's a bit young for me, though,' I say, realising Carrie is staring at me, waiting for a reply. 'I prefer an older man with more experience. Also, it's never a good idea to get involved with staff.'

Carrie doesn't answer and turns to look out of the window. I've managed to put my foot in it yet again. I seem to be doing it all the time lately. Why did I make that stupid remark about staff? It's something I'd say to my other friends – my rich friends – because it's the way they talk and I like to fit in. I sometimes forget I don't have to do that with Carrie. Although I don't know why she's still so chippy about everything, because she went to the same private school as me, even if she was there on a scholarship and I wasn't. I may be rich now, but I wasn't born that way, even though I like to give that impression. Carrie knows the truth about my background and it's one of the reasons we became best friends. I look out of the window and pretend to be fascinated with the passing streets. I can't change who I am, although I do try to be mindful that Carrie and I have very different attitudes to money. I hope it's not going to be one of those evenings where I'm frightened to open my mouth for fear of upsetting her.

'We're here.' Carrie has her hand on the door handle, ready to get out.

She sounds okay, not in a mood or anything so I smile at her, and we clamber out of the cab. We've barely got out of the door before it zooms off down the road.

'He was nice, wasn't he?' Carrie laughs and I relax. Tonight is going to be a good night; I just have to remember to think before I speak. Carrie can't help the way she is; she comes from a poor background and it's stayed with her. 'If he hadn't been prepaid, he might have been a bit nicer. There's something to be said for paying cash,' I say. I have no idea what it's like to be poor. Gramma used to call Carrie a communist and she didn't mean it as a compliment. It was a huge exaggeration, of course, and a typical Gramma remark, but it's true that Carrie thinks in a working-class, socialist type of way. I believe money is to be spent and enjoyed because life is short and who knows what's around the corner? Carrie believes money serves a purpose and shouldn't be squandered on things you don't really need.

She's a much better person than me.

The door to the gallery is wedged wide open and the gallery owner, my boss Sebastian, is standing in the doorway. He looks very handsome, if a little formal in a dark suit and crisp, white shirt. The black material of the suit contrasts starkly with his mop of wavy, blond hair and his perpetual tan highlights his perfect features.

'Mia. Carrie.' He steps out onto the pavement and air kisses us both, enveloping us in a cloud of expensive cologne. 'Marvellous of you both to come.'

'Well, I couldn't not, could I? Seeing as I work here.'

Sebastian laughs and makes a fuss of ushering us inside, telling us to help ourselves to a drink. I push Carrie forward to go in before me.

A dozen or so people are milling around and several are standing in front of one of the largest paintings, glasses of wine in hand. I spot the figure of Tally, the artist, deep in conversation with one of them.

'Is she giving them a sales talk?' I ask Sebastian quietly, watching as Tally waves her hand in front of a particularly horrible painting. He grimaces. Tally is everything he hates: loud, overly familiar and argumentative.

'They actually seem to like her,' he whispers in disbelief.

'I told you they would and when have I ever been wrong?' I ask.

'About paintings? Never,' he says, moving closer to me. 'But tell me this, why on earth did you bring the fun-sponge bookkeeper with you? You should have left her at home. Remember what she was like the last time?' I look at him, surprised to see a hint of anger on his face. 'You'd better make sure she keeps her opinions to herself and doesn't put the buyers off,' he continues.

Maybe I shouldn't have brought her. Carrie's come to lots of openings but at the last one, she got into a rather heated conversation with a would-be buyer about wasting huge amounts of money in the midst of a cost-of-living crisis. Sebastian wasn't around when it happened but someone must have blabbed to him. Tally, probably, because she's always lurking around and it's impossible for her to keep her mouth shut. As well as being an up-and-coming artist, Sebastian also employs her to help with the marketing because she was a whizz at it in a previous life, according to her. She's only supposed to work a couple of days a week, but she's here so often, it feels as if she lives here, and she never misses a thing.

'Sebastian,' I admonish playfully, placing my hand on his arm in an attempt to placate him. 'Of course she won't put anyone off, and remember she's my friend so play nice.'

His eyes lock onto mine and I feel the heat of his breath on my face as he moves even closer.

'Only,' he whispers, 'if you're nice to me.'

'I'm always nice. Aren't you?'

'Not always.'

I shiver as I feel his fingers trail slowly down my spine and I'm grateful that I'm standing with my back to the wall so no one else can see what he's doing. We hold each other's gaze and for a second; it's as if there is no one else in the room.

Until Carrie calls my name.

Sebastian sighs and I feel the increased pressure of his fingers on my back and I wince, staring at him in surprise. He drops his hand, the spell broken. I tear my eyes away from him to see Carrie glaring at me. I turn and saunter towards her, wondering if I'm imagining Sebastian's eyes burning into me as I walk away.

If only he and Carrie liked each other more. Or at all, actually.

They're poles apart; Sebastian is rich and privileged. Everything that she hates. Carrie is just, well, Carrie... and she makes no attempt to hide the fact that in her opinion, Sebastian's a spoilt little rich boy. I know that they only make a superhuman effort to be civil around each other because of me.

'That looked look very cosy,' Carrie mutters as we each take a glass of champagne from a passing waiter. Carrie won't drink hers; she'll take a tiny sip and then we'll swap glasses when I've finished mine.

'Just boring work stuff.'

'Looked a bit more than work stuff to me.'

I laugh dismissively, telling her not to be silly, but I can't ignore the little thrill that goes through me when I remember the feel of Sebastian's touch. There's a spark there: more than a spark.

Carrie glances over at Sebastian and then at me but as she opens her mouth to say something, I smile my brightest smile at Tally, who is making a beeline for us.

'Tally! How lovely to see you! Carrie's just been telling me how much she loves your paintings.'

Enveloping me and then Carrie in a hug, Tally launches full throttle into the story of the inspiration for her latest work. Carrie listens attentively and I sneak a glance at Sebastian.

He's studying me from the doorway, watching without even the tiniest hint of a smile.

And I like it.

3

Sebastian's asked me out for dinner, and I've said yes.

Is it a good idea to date your boss? Probably not, but as I don't actually need the job, it won't be a massive wrench if it all turns sour and I have to leave. Besides, it's just one date; it's not as if I'm going to marry him.

Life has been rather dull these past months. I'm not saying there haven't been men but my heart's not really been in it, not after what happened. It's been casual sex only, because none of them have interested me enough to make me want to see them again. Sebastian is hot and funny, if a little snobbish, and he knows how to enjoy himself – so where's the harm? He's not my usual type and that's exactly why I'm going to go out with him. He could be just what I need to get back to normal.

It happened as Tally's exhibition was winding down last week. I wasn't really surprised because we've been circling each other for months so perhaps it was inevitable. I think if Carrie hadn't been there on the opening night, Sebastian and I would definitely have got together then. And Carrie did enjoy the evening; for some bizarre reason, she likes Tally and was enthusiastic about her paintings. Thankfully, there was no talk from her as to whether buying art in the current financial climate was ethical and the evening went smoothly, with two of Tally's paintings reserved. The gallery's become quieter as the week's gone on and we've all become a little weary of it. Even Tally's seemed a bit bored by everything and hasn't been her usual garrulous self. Exhibition fatigue, I suppose.

So, there I was in the tiny back yard behind the gallery, basically hiding because I didn't want Tally to ambush me and start talking. It was fifteen minutes until we closed and it wasn't as if there was anything that needed doing so I didn't feel guilty. Sebastian appeared as if by chance but now I think about it, I'm sure he'd been watching me. He frowned at me and demanded to know what I thought I was doing. I stared at him like a rabbit caught in the headlights and he suddenly burst out laughing because he was joking, of course. We started chatting and somehow ended up in each other's arms and by the time we went back inside, everyone had gone, even Tally, who'd closed the door on her way out.

In the week since, work has been much more interesting than normal because there have been lots of secret lingering looks between Sebastian and I, with a definite undercurrent of sexual tension. I'm looking forward to tonight in a way that I haven't looked forward to anything since that night.

Since Marco.

There, I've thought about him and uttered his name in my head, and I haven't been struck down by a thunderbolt.

Marco.

Marco was so hot, he was practically on fire, but he wasn't in the slightest bit funny or snobbish; he was intense and dangerous – and I couldn't get enough of him.

I won't make that mistake again.

Anyway, enough of him; go away, Marco. I have to concentrate on the here and now. And, more pertinently, I have to tell Carrie that I have a date with Sebastian tonight. We never lie to each other so it's unthinkable that I'd go out on a date with him and not tell her. Although she wouldn't know because I'm out most evenings with various friends, so I *could* keep it quiet. She doesn't know about the casual hook ups I've had, for example. But as they were never going anywhere, they don't count, so I didn't feel obliged to tell her.

I'm not going to lie to her about Sebastian though, because I have a feeling we might be seeing a lot of each other. I've been putting off bringing it up all week but I'm definitely going to tell her when she gets home from work tonight.

Work on a Saturday... Honestly, who works on a Saturday?

Carrie, that's who. Luckily, I never have to work weekends as Sebastian employs an old friend of his, who actually wants to work on Saturdays. God knows why Carrie has to work though, because they're not even open to the public! I know she wants to progress in her career but she's an accountant, for God's sake; surely she could have the weekend off. I'd planned on speaking to her sometime today, dropping it casually into the conversation, but now I'm going to have to tell her in a rush and there won't be anything casual about it. As soon as she comes in, I'll just get it over and done with before I get ready to go out.

But if she's late, maybe I won't have to tell her at all.

Which I'm sort of hoping for because I know that she's not going to like it, not one little bit. But the minute I think this, I hear the sound of the front door opening and Carrie calling out hello.

Right, here goes.

I wander out into the hallway, putting on my brightest smile.

'Hi! Good day? I was just going to make a coffee if you want one?'

'Sounds good. I haven't stopped all day, ate a sandwich at my desk but couldn't even tell you what it tasted of, I stuffed it down so quickly.'

'Poor you, you must be exhausted. A coffee will perk you up.' I go into the kitchen and Carrie hangs her bag up and follows me.

'You seem very chipper,' she comments.

'Do I?'

'Yes, you do.' She raises an eyebrow.

'Well, I have a date tonight.'

'Oh, yes? Who with?'

'Sebastian.' Her face drops when she hears his name and she makes no attempt to hide it. 'I know you don't get on with him, but I like him. It's just a date, nothing serious.'

'Don't you think it's a bit soon, you know, after what happened?'

I want to laugh and tell her that Sebastian certainly wouldn't be the first but then I remember that she doesn't know about my other hook ups. They weren't what you'd call dates, they were simply fulfilling a need. Carrie may be my best friend but we're very different and unlike her, I can't live like a monk. Or a nun. Whatever, you get my drift.

'It's definitely not too soon. Marco was eight months ago; it's time to move on.'

'Okay.' She sits down. 'But is it a good idea to date the boss?'

I shrug. 'Like I say, it's just one date.'

She pulls a face and I feel suddenly irritated. I'm looking forward to tonight and now it's turning sour, surprise, surprise.

'Look, Carrie, I like him, okay? You don't have to like him but it would be nice if you could try.'

'It's not that.'

I give her a questioning look.

'I mean, you're right; I don't really like him, but I've heard stuff about him. Bad stuff.'

'Bad stuff?' I demand.

'He doesn't treat women well; just uses them and discards them. Thinks that because he's good-looking and rich, he can treat them like dirt. From what I've heard, he's been through a lot of the female artists at the gallery and quite a few of the customers, too.'

I laugh. 'I'm not marrying him, it's just a date and why shouldn't he go out with whoever he likes? He's single.'

'It's not just that.' She looks uncomfortable for a moment. 'Okay. I'm just going to say it; there's a rumour that he spiked one of the female artist's drinks at an exhibition.'

'What?' I look at her in disbelief. 'Sebastian? No, I don't believe it. Who told you that?'

'Someone who knows him.'

'Who?' I demand. 'Because you obviously believe them.'

'It was Tally.'

'Tally?' I laugh. 'You mean the biggest gossip in the world who makes stuff up? Honestly, Carrie, I can't believe you even listened to such rubbish.'

'Why would she lie?'

'Because she can't help herself! It's also sour grapes because Sebastian isn't the slightest bit interested despite her practically throwing herself at him. Honestly, Carrie, look at Sebastian; do you actually think he has to drug women to get them into bed?'

'There's no smoke without fire.'

'I'm not talking about this any more.' I flick the kettle off, all thoughts of making coffee forgotten, and head towards my bedroom, leaving Carrie alone with her ridiculous notions.

* * *

I'm having a nice soak in the bath before I go out, to relax me for the evening ahead.

I'm also avoiding Carrie and trying to calm down.

I feel really angry at her for what she said about Sebastian but now I'm thinking about it, the blame lies squarely with Tally. She's a horrific gossip, as well as being an absolute drama queen, and each time she tells a story, she embellishes it. Some of the absolute nonsense that I've heard from her since I started at the gallery beggars belief. She needs to be a bit careful because she's going to spout off to the wrong person one day. I don't believe for one second that Sebastian would spike someone's drink; it's complete, made-up drivel. I can't blame Carrie for believing Tally; she doesn't know her very well and the bald truth is that Carrie and Sebastian are never going to like each other and she's all too eager to believe the worst of him. I can't choose to go out with someone on the basis that everyone else likes them. Carrie never liked Marco, either, although in his case, she was absolutely right, and I wish I'd taken heed of her warnings.

I'm just going to relax and not overthink it or start justifying myself to her, or try to convince her of the truth about Tally. I'm an adult, after all. I close my eyes and breathe in the scent of the bubble bath; I'm determined to enjoy this evening. I'm a firm believer in living life to the full and grabbing it with both hands; life is short and you never know what's around the corner. I could be run over by a bus tomorrow and I know full well that nobody knows how long they're here for. Both of my parents were killed in a plane crash when I was very young and I had to go and live with Gramma, but she's dead now too, so doesn't that just prove my point?

I don't even remember my parents – although I have pictures of them. Isn't that tragic? I was nineteen months old when they died in an airplane crash, so have no memories of them at all. One thing I do know is that if I ever have children, I won't be jetting off on a week's holiday to Menorca without them. The strange thing is, if they'd still been alive, I wouldn't be rich – because they weren't. My parents were a normal couple with busy lives who were treating themselves to some time out. They were both well-insured but more than that, the airline was found culpable of neglect and the huge compensation payment they were forced to pay was invested for me and has grown each year. I know I should be grateful that I've been left very well provided for, but I'd rather have had loving parents to bring me up than a trust fund and an aging relative.

I open my eyes and face the fact that I'm not going to be able to relax. Time to get out of the bath and make myself beautiful.

* * *

'Why can't I come in?'

We're standing outside my apartment building and as soon as we got out of the cab, Sebastian sent it away.

I wish he hadn't done that.

'You just can't,' I say.

'It's your apartment, Mia,' he says, pulling me close and nuzzling my neck. 'You can have whoever you like in there.'

It is my apartment and if it were any other man than Sebastian, I'd invite them in but after the heated conversation with Carrie, I can't. When I left the apartment, I made no attempt to speak to her and although she must have heard me in the hallway, she didn't bother coming out of the lounge. I thought it best if we both calmed down after what had happened and also, I didn't want to have to listen to any more rubbish that Tally has been dripping into her ear. Who knows how long Tally's been poisoning Carrie against Sebastian? Maybe if she'd kept her big mouth shut, Carrie wouldn't dislike Sebastian so much.

'It's just awkward,' I say, pushing him away slightly. If he keeps on doing that neck-nuzzling, I might just invite him up anyway and ignore how Carrie will be about it.

He suddenly lets go of me and takes a step backwards. 'It's because of her, isn't it? Your big-chip-on-her-shoulder lodger. Honestly, Mia, I don't know why you put up with her. She's miserable and boring and is always waving her working-class credentials around like a banner. Plus, she behaves as if she's your mother.'

'She's not like that.'

'She's exactly like that.'

We stare at each other in the dim light coming through the glass doors of the building. We've had a wonderful evening and now it's all turned sour.

'I didn't realise you were only after sex, Sebastian.' I put on an affronted voice; this usually ensures immediate grovelling from a man, but not from Sebastian.

He sighs. 'Don't be ridiculous; you know it's not like that. We're adults, Mia. You want to continue our evening as much as I do.'

He's right. If it wasn't for Carrie's dislike of him, I'd have asked him in straight away.

'We could go to yours,' I suggest.

'It's a cab ride away and if you'd said before the cab left, we could have done. Anyway, funnily enough, I don't feel like it now. The thought of old fun-sponge bookkeeper loitering around has killed the moment.' He steps forwards and kisses me lightly on the lips and then draws back and stares at me.

'It doesn't matter, Mia; there'll be other nights. I don't want to spoil our evening by arguing about her. Go on in; I'm going to walk along to the bridge and grab a cab.'

'See you on Monday?' I ask, tentatively.

He takes hold of my face between his hands and kisses me deeply.

'You can count on it.' He releases me and then takes my hand and leads me to the door and presses the button on the wall. Owen appears within seconds and releases the door lock. He's arrived so quickly that it makes me wonder if he was watching us. He pulls the door wide open and after a last, lingering look at Sebastian, I go in.

'Did you have a good evening, Miss Enderby?' He smiles at me and I make myself smile back.

'Very nice, thank you.' I go straight over to the lift, get in and press the button. The door closes as Owen looks on, his face a picture of disappointment at my lack of conversation.

Looks as if I'm disappointing everyone today.

I quietly let myself into the flat and am surprised to see a light coming from the lounge. It's gone twelve o'clock and Carrie is normally in bed by now. Has she stayed up to try and convince me not to see Sebastian again or was she waiting to see if I brought him back? I feel suddenly exhausted... Why does everything have to be so difficult?

I open the lounge door to see Carrie sitting on the sofa in her pyjamas. She looks up and smiles.

'Nice evening?'

I stare at her in surprise; I wasn't expecting that. When I don't answer, she jumps up, comes over and puts her arms around me.

'I'm sorry about earlier, about the way I've been

about your date with Sebastian, but I'm just looking out for you.'

'I don't need looking out for. Tally's just a liar and a gossip and I can't believe you've been sucked in by her.'

'Look. I need to explain why I said what I did. Let's have a mug of cocoa and a chat like we used to after a night out, shall we? Remember how we used to talk for hours about the fun we'd had? Get comfy on the sofa and I'll go and make it, yeah?'

'Okay.' I don't want any cocoa but don't say so; I'm too tired to have another argument. 'I'll go and get ready for bed first.'

'Okay.' She heads towards the kitchen. 'Don't fall asleep,' she calls over her shoulder.

I go into my bedroom, quickly change into my pyjamas and wipe my make-up off before going back into the lounge. Carrie is back, sitting on the sofa with two mugs of cocoa on the coffee table in front her. I flop down next to her.

'I have some apologising to do, Mia.'

I wait.

'Maybe Tally was exaggerating; maybe she's a woman scorned and all that.'

'Maybe?' I give her a questioning look.

'And maybe I'm too ready to believe anything that shows Sebastian in a bad light.' She gives me a rueful smile. 'But all I'm doing is looking out for my best friend who I don't want to see getting hurt again. I'm sorry.'

I think about what she's said, and the silence stretches.

'You don't have anything to apologise for, Carrie,' I say, eventually. 'You weren't to know what Tally's like. If anyone should apologise, it should be me. What happened with Marco has made you overprotective. I'm so sorry that you had to deal with it all. It's not fair; you've done more for me than any friend should have to do...'

'Stop.' She puts her hand on my arm. 'You're my best friend and you know I'd do anything for you, but that doesn't give me any right to poke my nose in and tell you how to live your life.'

'You have every right,' I say. 'Because we both know that I've made so many stupid mistakes and without you to sort out my disasters, who knows where I'd be. Marco was the last in a long line of catastrophes and you must be sick of me. Now you have to carry the weight of what I did and if I'd listened to you in the first place, it never would have happened. I have to live with the guilt of what you had to do for me for the rest of my life and it's totally my own fault.'

'It wasn't your fault. Marco wasn't a good person.'

'That didn't give me the right to kill him. I'm such a bad person, Carrie.'

'He deserved it!' Carrie almost shouts and I stare at her in shock. 'I know you didn't mean to do it, but he was rotten through and through, and you just couldn't see it. He was an abuser and like all abusers, he made you think everything was your fault. He was a bully and if he hadn't been so twisted and vile to you, it would never have happened. Besides, what sort of idiot has a loaded gun lying around their flat?' Her cheeks are flushed with anger and she's almost out of breath.

'I thought I loved him,' I say, quietly.

'I know. And because of that, you were blinded to what he was really like. I knew the first time I met him he was trouble – I've met his sort so many times – but I couldn't make you see him for what he was.'

She couldn't, and she did try. Perversely, the more she took against Marco, the more attractive he became to me. He didn't fall at my feet like other men; I was the one desperate for him to love me, not the other way around. There was something dark and dangerous about him and I loved it. One compliment from Marco cancelled out a hundred of his insults. I couldn't get enough of him, or him me, although the only time I felt he truly cared about me was in bed.

'I failed you, Mia. I should have tried harder to make you see him for what he was.'

'You've never failed me. Never.' I take hold of her hands. 'You're the best friend anyone could ever have, and I don't deserve you.'

She smiles and we sit in silence for a while. Marco's taunting face on that night punches itself into my consciousness: his showing off with the gun, his insistence that he moved in dark places, whatever that meant. His refusal to tell me how he actually earned his money. He didn't work for a living, he told me with a smirk, as if work were a dirty word; he acquired money. Whatever that meant. All of the things that should have put me off him but didn't; it made him all the more fascinating. I find it incredible now that I was flattered by his jealousy and refusal to meet any of my friends; when he told me he didn't want to share me, I foolishly believed it meant that he loved me. I excused his physical intimidation as proof of his overpowering passion for me.

How stupid I was – how deluded.

If only we hadn't argued that night; if only that stupid gun hadn't been lying there. I was on edge before I had even arrived at his flat, as if I sensed something bad was going to happen. Carrie sensed it too; she tried to persuade me not to go and of course, the more she tried to persuade me, the more determined I became. Her increasingly frantic messages to me that went unanswered were the reason she turned up at Marco's. Thank God she did. If only I'd listened to her and never gone there on that night.

If only.

He told me the gun wasn't loaded; he told me, I'm sure he did. He must have truly believed that, or else he would never have dared me to pick it up. Why did I point it at him? Why did I pull the trigger?

'Carrie,' I say, quietly. 'I know you say it's better not to know where Marco is but I can't stop worrying that his body will be found and you'll be implicated because of me. Someone, somewhere, must be missing him, because he can't just disappear and no one notice that he's gone.'

She sits forward on the sofa and turns to face me. 'You don't need to worry. Marco was estranged from his family, remember? He told you he never saw them because I remember you saying that at least he had the choice, unlike you. He hated his parents, and his brother was just a kid when he left. He'd been backpacking around the world for so many years that anyone he was still in contact with will assume he's still travelling. It's taken care of; the odd text will be sent to give the illusion he's still around and eventually, people will lose interest and forget about him. He had no proper job to be missed from. You don't need to worry.'

'I can't help it. It all seemed too easy. For me. Twenty-five thousand pounds to make Marco go away and never bother me again. Twenty-five thousand pounds for a life; is that all he was worth? I feel so guilty about what happened; I still have nightmares about it. I didn't mean to kill him.'

Carrie doesn't speak but drinks her cocoa and I pick up mine and take a few gulps of the sickly sweetness. I should have just left it and accepted her apology about Sebastian but a part of me needs to know what she did. I need reassurance that it's not all going to come back to haunt us. To haunt me.

'How did you do it, Carrie? Who sorted it out? Who's sending texts from Marco's phone? What if they tell someone or they decide to blackmail us?'

She shakes her head, her expression serious. 'You don't need to worry, that's all I can say. The less you know, the better.'

I open my mouth to speak but take a gulp of cocoa instead; I need to stop asking. She's never told me any facts but I'm aware enough of her background to understand that she knows people who can fix things. Bad people. Carrie used her intellect at an early age to escape from that life by getting herself a scholarship to a private school. She never speaks of her family but has let slip that they're not good people; they exist and hide behind the dark web. She had to pay someone to fix my problem and she couldn't have done that without getting involved. Because of me, she's had to revisit her past and do something terrible.

'What I really wanted to say, Mia,' Carrie says, 'is that I've been overprotective of you and that's not right. We're the same age and I have no right to tell you what to do or who to see because you're an adult – not a child. Sebastian and I are never going to be best friends or see eye to eye because we're very different people, but he's not Marco. Tally is a gossip; I know that, and I shouldn't have believed her so easily. I just don't want you to get hurt again. I promise I won't keep trying to tell you how to live your life. I've overstepped the mark and I'm sorry.'

'You don't have to say sorry.'

'Well, I've said it now and I meant it, so let's not dwell on it any more.'

'Fine by me.' I smile, pleased that we can get back

to normal and I can see Sebastian without feeling bad, or having to lie about it to my best friend.

'Good.' Carrie chinks her mug against mine. 'So, here's to the future, and forgetting the past.'

I clink my mug against hers.

I'll definitely drink to that.

4

I open my eyes and immediately panic when I see only darkness.

Complete, pitch-black darkness.

I always have a night-light on, just a plug-in that sits in the socket by the dressing table and casts a dim light over the floor. Why isn't it on?

And then I hear it and my stomach flips.

You'll be sorry.

It's Marco's voice. I try to move but can't; I will my body to sit upright and get out of bed but I lie frozen, as if pinned to the bed by invisible hands.

You have to pay for what you've done, Mia... You have to pay.

His voice echoes around the room. He's in here

somewhere, hiding in the dark. Where is he? I can hear him breathing, deep, ragged breaths.

Or is it my own breathing that I can hear?

Stop it, Mia; it's a dream. I've having one of my nightmares and I'll wake up in a minute and everything will be fine. A loud rattling sound makes my heart jump in my chest, and I realise it's the bedroom door handle. I open my mouth to scream but nothing comes out except a choking sound.

I hear Marco's laughter from outside the door; the same cruel, mocking laughter that I remember from that night. The memory fires itself into my brain like a rocket; 'Trust fund girl', he'd sneered, 'did you really think I was interested in you? You stupid, spoilt bitch. You're a cash cow, that's all.' I force the memory away, close my eyes and wish that I could wake up.

It won't stop; the laughing is so loud that it echoes around the room. The door handle rattles again, and my heart rate is so fast, I must surely be about to have a heart attack.

Wake up, Mia, wake up!

I won't stop, Mia, I won't ever stop. He's banging on the door, loud thudding that must be real because how could I imagine a sound like that? I can feel the banging; it's moving the air in the room.

The thumping suddenly stops and I hold my breath.

Has he gone?

Then the door shakes and rattles and there's a thudding noise as if he's on the other side, throwing himself at it. The door is going to give way and he's going to get in any minute. He wants revenge and who can blame him? I open my mouth and this time, I manage to scream, long and loud. I squeeze my eyes tightly shut and when I hear the bedroom door open, I pray that whatever Marco is going to do to me will be over quickly. Cold fingers wrap themselves around the top of each of my arms and my insides turn to liquid.

'Mia! Mia!'

It's not Marco.

I open my eyes and stare into the concerned face of Carrie. The bedroom door is open and light is streaming in from the hallway.

'It's all right, Mia. You were having a nightmare.'

'No,' I whisper. 'He's here. He was in the hallway. I heard him.'

'No. It was just a nightmare, a night-terror. No one's here except for me and you. You've had a bad dream and it's not surprising after what we were talking about last night.'

I slowly pull myself upright. My hands are shaking and I'm shivering.

'It was so real and I couldn't see anything. I couldn't move. I heard him, Carrie, I heard him out there, laughing at me. Go and check. Please.'

Carrie takes hold of my hands. 'This is why we shouldn't talk about it any more. Your nightmares were getting better and now we've stirred it all up again and made it worse.'

I stare at her and with a sigh, she gets up and goes out into the hallway. Moments later, she's back.

'There's no one out there, Mia. There couldn't be; you know that. Marco's dead.'

'Maybe it's his ghost come back to get revenge for what I did.'

Carrie doesn't say anything and I realise how deranged I must sound but I can't seem to pull myself together.

'My night light wasn't on. It's always on; why isn't it working?'

She goes over to the dressing table and bends down in front of the night light. She stays there for a while, head bent, and then pulls the light out of the socket and brings it over to me.

'I think it's had it. Look, the plastic's all discoloured and yellow.' She holds it out to me. 'I had a job to pull it out of the socket because it was almost welded in there. How long has it been plugged in for?'

I shrug. 'I can't remember. Years, probably.'

'Things don't last forever, do they? You just need a new one, that's all. No mystery there.'

I start to feel calmer and my heartbeat slows, gradually returning to normal.

'It just felt so real. It sounded so much like him.'

'Well it would, wouldn't it? It's coming out of your head so it would sound exactly like him. It's because we were talking about it and dragging it all up again. It's guilt that's giving you nightmares, but you have to put it behind you. You can't change what's happened and that's why it's best not to keep raking it up all the time. Put it in a box and bury it.'

I wince when she says that because Marco could be buried in a box. Although that's what I always do: bury bad memories. It usually works. I know what Carrie is saying is right but the irrational part of me is still afraid.

'Are you okay? Do you think you'll be able to go back to sleep?'

'I'll be fine,' I lie. 'You go back to bed. Sorry I woke you up; what a baby, screaming like that. And what twenty-six-year-old is afraid of the dark? Pathetic.'

'You're not pathetic and we all have our phobias. You know what I'm like about spiders; it's no different.'

'You always make me feel better.'

'That's what friends are for,' she says softly. 'Are you sure you'll be okay?'

I nod.

'Okay. Well, I'll leave your door open and the hallway light on, all right?'

'Thank you.'

'No problem, sleep well, and remember, it was just a bad dream and dreams can't hurt you.' She goes out into the hallway, and I lie back down.

I close my eyes and pull the quilt up to my chin.

It was just a dream, Mia, so go back to sleep.

And grow up.

* * *

Imi, Maria and Suki are just what I need after last night; funny and slightly bitchy gossip, washed down with a few cocktails after a very edible lunch. We usually meet up at least once a week for a catch up and I sorely need a good laugh. Sunday is an unusual day for us to meet but it was the only day we could all manage this week.

We're in the Diamond Lounge, an ultra-modern bar next to the Suitors Restaurant where we've just had lunch. The place is on the edge of the country-side but still within easy reach of London. Normally, we stick to town but Suki wanted to show off her brand new Mercedes so offered to pick us all up so we could sit in her car and admire it. Suitors is quite select and not easy to get a table in unless you know the right people but as Imi's father owns it, there's always a table free for us. I tried to persuade Carrie to come too, as there was easily room for three of us in the back of the car, but she said no, she had some preparation to do for an important work meeting to-morrow. Imi, Maria and Suki were at the same school as us so it's not as if she doesn't know them; she wouldn't be having lunch with strangers. I just wanted her to get out a bit more and stop being such a hermit.

Although I have to admit, it is slightly easier without her.

Imi, Maria and Suki are all very well off, so I don't have to mind what I say about money or things like that. I can relax with them and the conversation is easy and light-hearted and not too in-depth or soul searching. None of us are hung up about class or money; maybe because we have both, or at least I appear to. I regale them with the details of my date with Sebastian, telling them how hot he is, although they've all met him at various art exhibitions so already know what he looks like. I think Imi is a little jealous because she's not saying a lot. Maybe she's embarrassed because she made a very obvious pass at Sebastian at an opening night earlier in the year and he rebuffed her, but the worst thing was that Maria witnessed it and told me and Suki. It probably stings a bit that I'm seeing him now.

I missed out the last part of the evening with Sebastian, obviously, because that was just a blip. They all ask what I'll do if it turns sour, what with working for him, and I tell them that I've already thought about this and should that happen, I'll just leave. My job isn't essential and working front-of-house at the gallery isn't exactly a career, although I do quite enjoy it. I won't have any trouble getting another job because I have lots of contacts – although a not very good degree – but hopefully it won't come to that.

I have a good feeling about Sebastian. We're very alike in a lot of ways and, if Marco taught me anything, it's that opposites may initially attract but they don't work. Too many differences. I immediately push the thought of him, and the nightmare last night, away.

In a box and buried.

I take another sip of my cocktail – my third – and concentrate on what Suki is saying to make sure Marco doesn't push his way into my thoughts again. Suki's regaling us with all the gory details of her breakup from her latest boyfriend. He's the reason she's treated herself to a new car; she says she deserved it after putting up with his moods and tantrums for six months. According to Suki, it's single all the way from now on.

I've heard it all before.

Give it a couple of weeks and she'll be giving every man she meets the come on, because she can't help herself. Maria suggests another cocktail and I say no and then quickly change my mind; why not? It's not as if I have to drive home and after last night, I need to relax and let myself go a bit. I'll have an early night tonight to recover from my broken sleep and the cocktails will have dissipated by then. They're mostly sugar, anyway, with very little alcohol in them.

I hope they don't make me dream.

And he's done it again: wheedled his way into my head.

Giving Maria my order for a Passion Fruit Martini, I pick up my handbag and head for the ladies room. The lounge has filled up since we came in and I have to weave my way through the throng to get to the restrooms on the far side of the bar. As I make my way through, I can feel admiring glances from several of the men I pass and I give one or two of them a lingering look just so they can see what they're missing. I'm a flirt, it's true, but where's the harm?

If you've got it, flaunt it, that's my motto, because looks don't last forever.

After I've washed my hands and applied another coating of lipstick and a quick squirt of perfume, I head back to the girls. My head feels a little woozy from the cocktails – I fear the barman may have been a little heavier on the alcohol than normal – but that doesn't stop me looking forward to my next one.

Maybe the alcohol will help me sleep tonight.

I stop and take a deep breath; *get out of my head, Marco Henderson, and stay out.* I take a step and walk purposefully forward, squeezing past a middle-aged couple deep in a conversation that sounds danger-ously close to an argument. Honestly, there are better places to have meaningful exchanges.

And that's when I see him.

He's striding confidently towards the exit doors,

weaving in and out of the crowd of people as he makes his way across the room.

It can't be him, the sensible part of my brain tells me; it can't, because he's dead.

He has the same jet-black, unruly curls, the same build: tall and slim, yet muscular. But more than that, it's the walk, Marco strides and holds his head in a certain way, almost regal. As if he's the most important person in the room, which he was, for me, for a while.

I stand and watch him for a moment and before I know what I'm doing, I've changed direction and am no longer going back to my table with the girls; I'm following him. Wending my way through the crowd, I think I've lost sight of him and then I see him again, getting closer to the exit. I've nearly caught up with him when a group of three men step right in front of me. I dodge to one side and one of them, a tanned six-footer in chinos and a crisp, white shirt, steps smartly in front of me and asks me if I'd like a drink. I step to one side and he matches my step and laughingly asks me if I want to dance. He's handsome and suave and has probably used that line on a thousand girls and received a smile in return. It may have even worked on me if I hadn't been in such a hurry. I scowl at him and snap 'Excuse me,' and he steps out of my way with a surprised look.

I hurry to the doors and just catch them as they're about to swing closed. I squeeze through and stare around the car park and see the figure that I've been following climbing into a large, black car. I watch as it starts up and pulls neatly out of the space, along the front of the car park and onto the main road. I stand for several moments and watch it disappear into the distance.

I feel like a complete idiot as what I've just done dawns on me; I've chased a dead man.

What was I thinking?

I need to get a grip on myself because I've followed someone who I thought was Marco and, as I very well know, Marco is dead.

I need to put him out of my head otherwise I'll drive myself mad.

The dead can't come back, and they can't hurt you.

5

'I suppose we should get up.' Sebastian props himself up on one elbow and gazes down at me.

'It's only eight o'clock.' I turn to face him. 'We could stay here for a while,' I say in my best seductive voice.

He pulls a face. 'As much as I'm tempted, knowing that Carrie is up and about is a bit of a passion-killer.'

'The walls are thick; she won't hear us.'

He sits up and swings his legs over the side of the bed.

'I can't,' he says with a rueful grin. 'The thought of your lodger with her ear against the wall is too much.'

I laugh guiltily. 'She wouldn't! And she's not my lodger; she's my friend and flatmate.' Okay, so she doesn't pay rent, but I don't tell him that. I don't need the money, so why would I make her pay?

Sebastian stands up and stretches and I lie back and admire him, which, obviously, is why he's doing it. He's what Gramma used to call 'a fine figure of a man'. He sits back down on the bed and pulls his boxers on, his back to me.

'She is your lodger; this is your apartment, isn't it? So, she's your lodger. Why doesn't she get her own place? She could afford to rent somewhere on her own but chooses to live in your spare room. She's just weird, Mia, but you can't see it.'

I sit up, pull the quilt around me and watch as he pulls his clothes on.

'Why don't you like her?'

He stops and turns around to face me.

'She's odd. Honestly Mia, I can't fathom why you're friends with her. She has a massive chip on her shoulder about money and class and she doesn't even try to hide it. She doesn't fit in with people like us and I can't understand why you bother with her. She's hard work and drains all the fun out of the room with her working-class hang ups.'

'Ouch,' I say. 'Remind me never to cross you.'

He shrugs. 'I'm just telling it how I see it.'

'You're a massive snob, Sebastian, that's the problem.'

'So are you Mia, when it comes to anyone else. What's so different about her?'

'She's been such a good friend to me, you have no idea. We've been best friends since we were twelve and have always been there for one another.'

He plumps the pillows and then swings his legs up onto the bed and stretches out.

'Okay, tell me why she's such a good friend. I'm all ears. Maybe you can make me understand why you put up with her.'

I settle back and keep my voice low even though I wasn't lying when I told Sebastian that the walls are thick. I feel awkward and disloyal talking to him about Carrie when she's in the apartment.

'We met at school; she was on a scholarship and arrived on my twelfth birthday. I felt sorry for her because everyone else just ignored her. She spoke differently and came from a different background. I suppose you could say I took her under my wing.'

Sebastian leans across and kisses me. 'Too kind-hearted, that's your trouble.'

I smile and take the compliment but it's not the entire truth; I felt just as much of an outsider as

Carrie did, although no one would ever have believed it because I'm very good at pretending that I'm fine, even when I'm not. I was an orphan and whilst plenty of my peers came from broken homes, I was the only one without any parents at all. Some of the more spiteful girls picked up on that and made it their mission to make barbed comments to me to try and get a reaction. The jealously I felt when they goaded me by boasting about their homes and families was nearly overpowering. On several occasions, I'd given vent to that jealousy. By the time Carrie arrived at the school, although the things that I'd done weren't attributable to me – because I was very clever about who I took revenge on for being so horrible to me – I knew it was only a matter of time before I went too far. I knew that if I carried on, slapping and pinching and being generally spiteful weren't going to be enough to escape my feelings. My emotions were so out of control that I was dangerously close to doing something so bad that I'd be expelled. I had no one to confide in, no one that I trusted enough to tell how I was struggling. Until Carrie.

'Despite our differences, we became really close. Carrie is very kind and caring and yes, she is serious, but that's not surprising, given her background. It's only through sheer determination that she's been able to make something of herself. And as you know, the only family I had was Gramma, and she wasn't the maternal type.'

Gramma wouldn't have Carrie in the house; she was an even worse snob than Sebastian. Although she was a poor snob until I came along and she took care of me and my trust fund, which made her worse, I think. Gramma had met Carrie on a few occasions at the school when she visited, and they'd barely spoken but just the fact that she was a scholarship girl was enough for Gramma to dislike her. When I asked if Carrie could come and stay for the school holidays, she wouldn't countenance it; wouldn't even talk about it. I had to suffer her cold silence for several days afterwards for having the temerity to even ask. Which turned out to be a waste of time anyway because when I told Carrie and apologised for Gramma, she said she wouldn't have come anyway.

'So how did Carrie get on with the rest of your friends at school? Was she as chippy then as she is now?'

'No, she was fine,' I lie. 'Not everyone is as stuck up as you.'

He grins at me. He knows I'm not telling the truth, but I don't make any effort to convince him. Aside from me, Carrie never made any true friends because mostly, the other girls ignored her; treated her as if she wasn't even there. It was how the scholarship girls were treated and why most of them failed to stay until sixth form. But no one was outright nasty to her – although I don't think Carrie would have cared if they were. She has an inner strength and confidence in herself. She took me under her wing as much as I took her under mine, and she did far more for me than I ever did for her.

More than any friend should have to do.

A long-buried memory pops up and before I can force it down, it explodes into my head. A feeling of overwhelming rage engulfs me, and Charlotte, one of the most popular and bitchy girls in the school, flashes in front of my eyes with blood pouring from her face.

Screaming. Loud, loud, screaming.

I knew that I'd gone too far. That this time, there was no going back.

But Carrie saved me; risked everything for me by lying. Two liars' words against one telling the truth. The head knew we were both lying but she couldn't prove it and I got away with it. It taught me a lesson, though. After that, I managed to rein in my jealousy and pain at the loss of my parents because I knew that I wouldn't get away with it a second time.

'Is that it, then?' Sebastian asks, bringing me back to now. 'You befriended her and have been stuck with her ever since?'

'Oh, shut up, snooty pants.' I stretch out to him and slap him playfully, the duvet falling around my waist as I do so. I see Sebastian's gaze travel downwards.

'Are you sure you want to get up so early?' I ask, pushing the duvet even further down.

'Maybe not.' He slips his arms around my waist and pulls me closer. 'If you're sure she can't hear?'

'Of course she can't.' We kiss deeply and he lets go of me, stands up and I lay back and watch as he takes off his boxers.

I sigh with relief. Thank God for that: no more awkward questions.

* * *

We're on our second lap of the park and the coffee shop is beckoning. I've managed to drag Carrie out of the house for a Saturday afternoon walk with the promise of a coffee and cake afterwards. She tried to tell me she was working but I refused to take no for an answer. It's not healthy being cooped up all of the time, especially on such a lovely, sunny June day.

Once she could see I wasn't going to go away, she put on her trainers and off we went.

I'd rather have gone shopping, if I'm honest, but Carrie has this thing about sustainability and not wasting resources so sees clothes shopping as pointless and boring. The park seems like the safest bet because we can both get some fresh air, too.

We're so different and there's nothing wrong with that. Carrie always scrutinises every bill that we get whereas I stuff them into a drawer and don't even bother opening them. She's the one who collects the post from our post box in the foyer; if it wasn't for her, I wouldn't even see any of it and the box would be overflowing. I always promise myself that I'll look at them later but I never do; if anything looks vaguely official or financial, I shove it away and put it all in a bag at the end of the year and give it to my accountant to sort out. Everything is paid by direct debit so what's the point? It's all mind-numbingly tedious and boring; God knows how Carrie does it for a job.

'Are you seeing Sebastian tonight?' Carrie's tone is light. She's really making an effort, but I know it is an effort; her and Sebastian are never going to be the best of friends. I love her for trying, though, and this morning wasn't too bad, although it was still a relief when Sebastian left. They were perfectly polite to each other and Carrie even offered him a cup of tea, but it was awkward and stilted. I keep reminding myself that it's early days.

'No, not tonight. He's having dinner with a couple of his cousins, so I won't see him. Don't want to overdo it,' I say with a grin. 'Or meet his family just yet, although he did invite me along. I'm meeting up with Anna for dinner.'

Sebastian and I went out for dinner on Wednesday night but it wasn't a late one and he didn't stay over. We see each other every day at work and always find time for a bit of alone time – nothing sordid, because I'm not into office sex – but I have my other friends too and I'm not going to ditch them to spend every minute with him.

I'm taking it slowly.

This time.

'Come on,' I say, increasing my pace and speeding up. 'Race you to the coffee shop. Last one buys the cakes.'

I power along and Carrie hurries to catch me up. We giggle as we attempt to outrace each other without breaking into a run. If only I could outrun the spectre of Marco, my life would be perfect. I push open the door to the coffee shop and drop into the seat at the first empty table.

'Beat you!' I call as Carries strides in behind me. She grins, goes up to the counter and places our order, her cheeks flushed from the exertion. Drinks ordered, she comes over and flops into the seat opposite. Several people turn to look at us briefly before returning to their muted conversations. The place is packed – not surprising for a Saturday.

'What plans do you have for tonight then?' Carrie looks around with a frown. 'I'm gasping. I hope those coffees don't take forever.'

'Like I said, I'm meeting up with Anna. Drinks then dinner at her friend's new restaurant in Mayfair.'

'Nice,' Carrie says. 'Remind me who Anna is?'

'We were at university together. I think you met her once when she stayed at the apartment for a few days. Tall, blonde.'

Carrie shrugs. 'Maybe. I don't remember her. You know what my memory is like.'

They have definitely met; I distinctly remember it. We all went out to a club together and got gloriously drunk and Carrie stayed in bed the whole of the next day because she had such a bad hangover. She was never much of a drinker, even in her student days. Carrie and I went to different London universities so lived in the same apartment as we live in now, although Carrie lived in halls for her first year. I rarely see Anna now; as soon as she obtained her degree, she jetted off to Switzerland to make her millions. We only meet up when she pops back to the UK occasionally to visit her family. For a while though, we were close friends.

'You could come out with us tonight,' I suggest. 'Have dinner with us. Reminisce the night we went to Jangles and you got wasted.'

Carrie laughs and then groans. 'Oh God, I remember now. I drank so much.'

'You did, even more than me, I think. Why don't you come tonight?'

'I'd love to but I can't; I really have to catch up on the work I've missed today.'

'You work too hard, Carrie. You shouldn't have to work weekends.'

The waitress appears with our coffees and cakes and places them on the table in front of us.

'I have to,' she says, once the waitress has gone. 'There's so much competition where I am it's the only way to progress. It'll all be worth it eventually and then I'll be working normal hours and making my minions work weekends.'

I murmur agreement as if I know what she's talking about and pick up my carrot cake and take a bite. I don't need to work, so progressing holds no interest for me. I go to work because if I didn't, I'd clatter around aimlessly all day and probably end up a hugely fat alcoholic.

'I need the loo before I can even think about drinking that latte.' Carrie stands up and heads towards the toilets at the back of the café and I take a tentative sip of my mocha. Far too hot; the barista has probably completely ruined it and I won't be able to drink it for about a week. I nibble on my cake and scan around the room, people-watching. Every table is occupied and there's the low buzz of conversation and the occasional screech of a child. God knows why anyone would bring a child in here; it's not exactly child friendly with it's hard-backed chairs and tiny tables with limited space. I'm just wondering if there's a queue for the ladies, as I could do with a visit myself, when my breath catches in my throat.

Marco is sitting at a table across the other side of the room. He has his back to me but I'd know that hair anywhere. I hold my breath and try to quell the rising feeling of panic. The rational part of me attempts to persuade my brain that it cannot be him but it's fighting a rapidly losing battle.

'That's a relief.' Carrie slips into the chair opposite. 'Must be all that walking.'

I don't answer, my eyes transfixed on the back of Marco's head.

'What's wrong, Mia?' she asks. 'Are you feeling okay?'

I open my mouth to tell her to look at Marco but in that moment, he stands up and turns around to leave.

It's not him; he's absolutely nothing like Marco. The panic eases from my body and I turn to face Carrie. I seriously need to do something about this: the nightmares, imagining that Marco is still here, the ridiculous idea that he's haunting me.

I think I need to talk to someone, a therapist maybe, but how can I? I can never tell the truth. It would be the same as last time. Almost.

'You're deep in thought.' Carrie looks at me with concern.

'I'm fine, just tired.'

'I'd ask why you're tired, but I don't think I want to know.' Carrie laughs and I somehow manage to laugh with her. She obviously thinks Sebastian and I were having sex all night and got no sleep at all.

Not so.

Of course we had sex, several times actually, but that's not the reason I'm tired. Sebastian quickly fell asleep, snoring softly beside me in his well-mannered way and I could so easily have drifted into a deep slumber but every time I almost dozed off, I opened my eyes again with a jolt.

What if I had a nightmare?

What if I woke up screaming as I have done several times this week? None of the nightmares have been quite as bad as last Saturday's, but they've been bad enough to wake Carrie. Screaming and sobbing that I've seen a dead man is hardly a good look, is it? What on earth would Sebastian think of me if he had to witness that?

But more to the point, what if he wanted to know who Marco was?

6

Hump day, that's what Wednesday is called, isn't it? The middle of the week, the hump you have to get over to ski down towards the weekend.

I'm seeing Sebastian tonight. We're a couple of weeks in and have settled into seeing each other several nights a week: the pre-we're-in-a-relationship stage. We're staying overnight at his place tonight. As he puts it, he has no flatmate to consider, no one to bump into whilst walking stark naked into the kitchen to get a glass of water in the middle of the night.

Not that he's done that; if there have been any glasses of water to be got, I've got them. I think the real reason he wants to stay at his is because the effort of being polite to Carrie is too much for him. And her. It's sweet that they're both trying so hard for my benefit but tonight will be much easier at Sebastian's. He's lured me there with the promise of cooking me dinner but we both know his real motive. I like Sebastian; I do. He's not the love of my life, but who knows how I'll feel in the future. I'm beginning to think that maybe I should start looking at men as possible life-partners, rather than just as exciting interludes.

I glance at my watch: eleven-thirty. The gallery is deathly quiet; only Tally is knocking about, loudly musing whether any of her paintings need repositioning when she should really be on the phone doing her marketing job of drumming up would-be customers.

I'm doing my best to ignore her. I haven't forgiven her what she said to Carrie about Sebastian and want to avoid talking to her if possible. I find her obnoxious on a normal day without knowing the absolute rubbish that she's spouting to people about Sebastian. I considered telling him about her but couldn't see what good it would do. Tally would deny everything and it could result in making Carrie look like a liar so I decided not to say anything. I think most people take what Tally says with a pinch of salt after talking to her for a while. When I think back to some of the stories she's told me about her friends and family, they sound completely made up. I've tried to remember if she's ever said anything to me about Sebastian but can't recall anything. I usually switch off after a while of her incessant talking.

I'm meeting Jake Matinson for lunch. He's an up-and-coming artist who Sebastian has been cultivating and is keen to get onboard before he becomes too popular and only wants to pay us a miniscule commission for the privilege of selling his paintings. My job is to convince him that we're the best and get him to commit to a date to come in and sign on the dotted line. I don't think he'll need any persuading at all though, because he's still a bit green around the ears. Nevertheless, I'll do the required wooing over a vegan lunch at Chester's Vegan Bowl.

I'm not meeting him until one o'clock but I'm bored and Tally is irritating beyond belief. More to the point, I need a walk because my mind won't settle. I pick up my handbag and jacket and pop my head around Sebastian's door to let him know that I'm off. He's on the phone listening to someone so doesn't speak but gives me a little waggle of his fingers. I head out of the doors, turn right and march towards the park.

Chester's Vegan Bowl is a twenty-minute walk away but before I go there, I need fresh air and a change of scenery. I wander around the park, dodging the prams and joggers, and find myself an empty bench to sit on. I breathe in the scent of newly mown grass and the faint sweetness of flowers and try to centre myself.

The nightmares and imagining seeing Marco around every corner are getting to me and I need to do something about them but have no idea what. The only person I can talk to is Carrie, but when we do talk about Marco, it seems to make things worse. I know perfectly well that he's dead, but my brain won't seem to accept it.

I have to do something, because I absolutely cannot have a repeat of what happened after Gramma died.

I was a mess.

Thankfully, it was only for a brief period but for those few weeks, I had absolutely no control over my life. The doctors called it a breakdown due to grief over losing Gramma and before I knew it, they were making decisions about what was best for me. The swiftness of it was terrifying; one minute, I was a functioning, adult member of society, the next, I had no rights at all. Even though everyone assured me they had my best interests at heart, it didn't feel that way. It felt as if I was fighting to prove my sanity so I could take control of my own life again.

It's no wonder my degree was so lacklustre; it's incredible that I managed to complete it at all.

I shudder.

I need to pull myself together. Quickly. All I can think about is Marco; even if I manage to push the thought of him away and stop imagining every dark-haired man that I see is him, I've no peace at night because he's constantly invading my dreams. It's making me preoccupied and slightly miserable and that's due in no small part to not sleeping. I'm exhausted. I was even rude to Owen this morning because of it; as soon as I got out of the lift, he made a beeline for me and tried to engage me in conversation and I just wasn't feeling it, I'm afraid. I more-or-less blanked him and, as I strode by, I couldn't fail to see the expression on his face. I felt really mean. He's always so pleased to see me and maybe I should find his fascination with me flattering but, to be honest, I find it irritating and slightly creepy. Jim, the other regular doorman, who has been on the front desk forever, is never anything but polite and rather formal and I must say I prefer that. It's almost a relief when Owen isn't on shift and it's Jim or one of the agency casuals who seem to change every week. Nevertheless, although Owen's not an actual friend, it's always been a policy of mine to be nice to people wherever possible. Gramma was always perfectly horrid and condescending to people who she referred to as 'the help', and I vowed that I'd never, ever, be like her.

I glance at my watch to see that it's nearly half-past twelve. I can't believe that nearly an hour has passed with it all whirling through my brain – did I fall asleep for a while without realising it? It's possible; I'm that tired. I stand up, smooth down the back of my dress and take a deep breath.

That's decided it; tonight, I'm taking a sleeping tablet.

* * *

Jake could talk for England, as Carrie would say. On and on, he droned: where his inspiration came from, who he admired, how he was going to be the next big thing. I had to butter him up, of course, tell him that he was a breath of fresh air in the current climate, blah, blah, blah. All the stuff we say to all the artists we want to sign. We always interlace it with subtle warnings of talented artists who didn't quite make it, the ones who outpriced themselves early on and sank without trace, never to be heard of again.

We don't want them getting an over-inflated sense of their own worth and thinking they can lower our commission.

By the time the overlong lunch had concluded, I'd arranged a date for him to come in to see Sebastian and sign the contract, so it was a successful, though tedious, few hours. At the end of the meeting, Jake asked if I would sit for him, and I wondered how long it was going to take him to ask me out. I replied that I'd think about it and let him know. I have to keep him sweet until he's locked into the contract but no way will he be painting me, absolutely not. His art is a mishmash of oils and mixed media with bits of newspaper or old books stuck onto the canvas and all of his portraits have a hint of a poor man's Salvador Dalí. I have no intention of being depicted in that manner.

By the time I left the restaurant, it was nearly four o'clock and I wandered back to the gallery enjoying the sunshine. Having made the decision to take a sleeping tablet tonight, I feel better for taking action and nipping this anxiety or whatever it is in the bud. When I arrive at the gallery, I'm dismayed to see Tally sitting in my place at reception with her feet up on my desk. She looks up with a bright smile and a loud 'Hiya' and I realise that I'm going to have to put up her with her until we close at five. She's only employed two days a week but she seems to be here constantly. I try to remember what days she works, but can't; she obviously doesn't have a life. Why doesn't she go home and paint some more of her awful paintings, instead of hanging around here all day?

'Lovely out, isn't it?' she says.

'It is.' I tuck my jacket underneath the desk. 'You should take a spin around the park before the sun goes down.' *Go away. I don't want to talk to you.*

'I can't,' she says, leaning back in my chair. 'I haven't got any protection on. I'll burn.'

I don't doubt it; Tally is one of those milky-white people who look as if they live their entire lives in a cellar.

'Do you want your seat back?' She looks up at me.

'Please.' I stand in front of her.

She slowly swings her legs off the desk and stands up. I sit down, glide myself up to the desk and pull open the drawer to pretend I'm going to start work. She stands and watches.

Go away.

'I hear you were meeting Jake Matinson.' She

perches on the edge of the desk and makes herself comfortable.

I smile. So that's why she's been hanging around. She's fishing; Sebastian never reveals who we might be considering taking on until it's a done deal.

'He was the year above me at art school.'

I say nothing; I daren't. She must have overheard Sebastian talking – she's always snooping around and eavesdropping. Or maybe Jake's been shooting his mouth off, even though we ask our prospective artists not to. I can't give her even the slightest hint that I've been out for lunch with him.

She sighs and twists one of her long plaits around her fingers. 'It's been so quiet here today. So boring. Only three customers in since you've been gone. I thought that one of them was going to buy one of mine, but they opted for one of Archer's in the end.' She pulls a face and I stifle a smile. The artists are all so jealous of each other and make no attempt to hide it. 'I spent ages talking to them, too. Honestly, some people have no taste. Although, actually, they wanted something small for the downstairs khazi so Archer's is probably a much better fit.' She gives a hoot of laughter and I keep my face impassive. Tally likes to drop slang into her conversation, thinking that it makes her sound up to the minute and relevant.

'Sebastian had someone in with him for over an hour earlier,' she says, dropping her voice an octave as if imparting a state secret. 'Shut in his office with the door closed. Deep in conversation, they were. Didn't even introduce us when the man left. He was hot, too, I mean really hot. I wouldn't have minded getting his number. Just my type: tall, dark and dangerous looking...'

'Mia?' Sebastian has appeared behind Tally and she turns and looks at him but doesn't move. 'Shall we go into my office?'

He wants to know how the meeting went.

'Sure.' I stand up and follow him. The disappointed look on Tally's face is the last thing I see as I close the office door.

Sebastian flops into his seat and I sit down opposite him.

'God,' he says, with a grimace. 'She's an absolute witch. She was asking you about Jake, wasn't she? She's already asked everyone else, although none of them know. How does she find out?'

'God knows,' I say with a laugh. 'She doesn't miss a thing. Anyway, it's a done deal; he's coming in to sign the contract on Friday.'

'Brilliant.' His face breaks into huge smile. 'I knew you'd clinch it.'

'I aim to please.'

'I'd kiss you,' he says, softly. 'But Tally's probably hovering outside the door, spying.'

I turn around and look through the small window in the door to see swift movement followed by a light clunk.

'I think she heard you.'

'Perhaps we should really give her something to gossip about,' Sebastian says with a wolfish grin.

'Maybe. But first you have to prove you can cook.'

* * *

Sebastian can indeed cook; he's proved that without a doubt. He whipped up a complicated chicken dish – I forget the name – with perfect Dauphinoise potatoes and green beans whilst still managing to look cool and elegant. The table was laid perfectly with shiny cutlery and sparking glasses, and he wouldn't even let me help clear up afterwards. I was very impressed; even when he told me that he'd attended a week-long culinary school to learn the basics of cooking and the chicken dish that he cooked for me was the culmination of that week's learning.

Even so, at least he can cook; I don't even try. As I say to Carrie, when she tries to tell me I need to learn: there are far too many good restaurants in the world to waste time cooking. I can toast bread and boil an egg if I'm really pushed and that's good enough for me. Except for going out to eat, I mostly exist on fruit and vegetable smoothies which I make job lots of and keep in the fridge for several days. They require no cooking, just a little chopping and a good whizz in the blender. They're healthy and have all of the nutrients I need, and I can pop one into my bag when I go to work to have for my lunch, so who needs to cook? Not me. Carrie thinks they're beyond disgusting and refuses to drink them, but I've acquired quite a taste for them.

So. We had a lovely evening and after dinner, we enjoyed finishing a bottle of very good wine and settled down on the sofa to watch a movie on Netflix. Neither of us were really concentrating and once we started kissing, we gave up on the movie halfway through and went to bed early. Not to sleep at first, obviously, because Sebastian is far too hot for that. When the time did eventually come to go to sleep, I slipped off to the bathroom and took one of my sleeping tablets. I've had the packet for an age but only ever taken them once and that was after Gramma died. They're not even mine; they were Gramma's. She had a cupboard full of drugs of all descriptions and I've kept them. Gramma believed in a drug for everything: drugs to make you sleep, to cheer you up, to wake you up, to calm you down. They're probably out of date now but I'm still hoping they'll do the trick. Anyway, I swallowed one down with a few mouthfuls of water and hoped for the best.

Sebastian was already asleep when I got back to the bedroom so I climbed into bed and lay there trying to think of anything but Marco. He kept trying to push his way in and I kept pushing him out and at some point, I fell asleep.

And that was it.

I woke this morning to the sound of Alexa telling us it was six-thirty and the feel of Sebastian cuddling up to me. The relief was immense: no nightmares and no screaming at the ghost of Marco. As I gave myself in to Sebastian's advances, I congratulated myself on finding the answer to my problem. I felt slightly hungover – not sure if that was the wine or the sleeping tablet – but I was just so relieved to know that I could get a good night's sleep again without those horrific nightmares.

Such a simple thing: a sleeping tablet. All that overthinking and drama and all I needed was drugs.

7

Sebastian and I went to the theatre last night but we
didn't spend the night together because he had a su-
per-early morning breakfast meeting with an Asian
client on Zoom. I came home to my apartment and
he stayed at his.

Which is just as well because I had the most
awful nightmare and managed to wake up Carrie
with my screaming.

This was despite taking a sleeping tablet before I
went to bed.

Now that I think back over last night, the signs
were there even before we got to the theatre; I was on
edge. I can't quite put my finger on why or even when
I began to feel like it and it must have been a gradual

build-up because I can't pin it to any specific moment or anything that sparked it. I felt buoyant and optimistic after staying the night at Sebastian's and marvelled at how different I could feel after a good night's sleep. I went home after work to get showered and changed and I was looking forward to the theatre because I rarely go these days.

But now I can't even remember what play it was we were watching.

Carrie wasn't home when I got in, which I remember feeling disappointed about because I wanted to tell her about the sleeping tablets and how successful they'd been. But she often works late – far too late – so I got showered and started to get ready to go out.

Maybe it was being on my own, I don't know. I'm not usually bothered about being alone; I was brought up by Gramma and she only spoke to admonish me, so I'm used to my own company. But I do remember starting to feel unsettled. I shook the feeling off and told myself to get a grip and got dressed, did my hair and make-up, picked up my bag and wrap and headed down to the foyer. It was only when I got out of the lift and looked at my watch that I realised my cab wasn't due for another fifteen minutes and I was far too early. That confused me quite a bit because I'm never early; I'm either right on the nose or running a few minutes late. If Owen or Jim are on shift, they always have to tell the cab to wait for me. So that was the first bit of oddness, nothing major but it was disconcerting and unlike me.

Things went rapidly downhill from then onwards.

Owen was sitting behind the desk but he didn't bound out from behind it as he normally does when he sees me; he looked up and instead of his trademark grin, he just stared at me, and not in a friendly way. I smiled at him and said hello and he stood up slowly, said, 'Good evening, Miss Enderby,' without cracking a smile and pressed the button to open the door. He didn't look happy at all and I remember feeling irritated that he'd totally overreacted to my slight rudeness the other day. It also meant that I'd have to go and wait outside now that he'd opened the door and was being so awkward. I strode past him and went straight outside and walked down the street to the corner and stood in front of an estate agents looking in the window. I started to feel a little angry at Owen then but, more than that, I couldn't shake off the feeling that his unsmiling face very much reminded me of Marco's.

Meaning that Marco was in my head before I even arrived at the theatre.

I wandered up and down in front of the estate agent's window for what seemed like forever and when I saw the cab coming down the road, I swiftly walked back to the apartment building. I didn't turn my head and look through the glass doors to see if Owen was looking out; if he wanted to be formal and miserable, then so could I. I got in the cab and we zoomed off. I tried to zone out the cab driver. He was a talker: one of those that keep up a constant monologue of chatter that requires no interaction from the passenger. I stared out of the window and tried to get back the good feeling that I'd had earlier in the day but it proved elusive; all I felt was nervous and agitated.

When I arrived at the theatre, Sebastian was waiting for me in the foyer and although I pretended to be pleased to see him, I just wanted to run away and hide.

But not at my apartment, because the thought of going back there and being on my own terrified me. I felt sick at the thought of being alone. I tried to act normally to Sebastian and hide the way I was feeling and once we were seated and the curtain went up; it should have been easier, but it wasn't. I have no idea what the play was about because I couldn't concentrate on it long enough to find out. I became utterly convinced that someone was watching me from the row behind and imagined that I could feel their eyes on me the entire time I was sitting there.

When the interval came, Sebastian had pre-ordered drinks in the bar so after saying I'd meet him there, I went to the ladies to freshen up. As I got up from the seat, I scanned the row behind me and no one was even looking at me.

But that didn't make me feel any better.

And then I saw Marco.

Obviously, it wasn't him, it couldn't have been him, but he must have a double. I'd walked along towards the ladies – there was a long queue with it being the interval – and there he was, just coming out of the men's toilets. I stopped in my tracks for a moment and watched as he headed down towards the stalls. After I'd recovered my wits, I followed him. There were so many people milling about that I had to weave my way around them and I lost sight of him several times. The audience were starting to take their seats again for the second half and I realised that time had somehow jumped around and Sebastian would be wondering where the hell I'd got to. Even knowing that, I was still determined to find

Marco's doppelganger, just to prove to myself that he has a double.

I couldn't find him.

The theatre was so full of people, it was impossible. It was as much as I could do to find my way back to my own seat again and by the time I did, the second half of the play had started and Sebastian was sitting in his seat, waiting. When he asked where I'd been, I lied and told him that someone had fainted in the ladies and that I'd stayed to help.

I think he believed me.

The feeling of being watched didn't stop and I remember closing my eyes at one point to try and centre myself. Maybe I had them closed for too long because when I opened them, Sebastian was staring at me with a puzzled expression on his face. I smiled at him and he smiled back but it felt awkward. After that, I caught him glancing at me out of the corner of his eye several times, as if I was being a bit odd. And I did keep looking around at everywhere except the stage, so that didn't help, I probably did look strange. But the worst thing was that even though I knew Sebastian had noticed and kept glancing at me, I couldn't seem to stop myself.

* * *

I'm feeling better today than I did at the theatre, though. Despite the lack of sleep and the awful nightmare, I feel calmer. I'm so exhausted from my disturbed sleep that I almost didn't come into work this morning. It was only the thought of spending the day in the apartment on my own that propelled me out of bed and into the shower. I couldn't face so much as a cup of coffee before I left home and thankfully, an agency casual was on shift so I didn't have to endure Owen's sulking.

The gallery has been busy this morning so I haven't had time to dwell on my weird behaviour last night. Sebastian and I shared a cab back to my place after the theatre and, although he's far too well-mannered to comment on my strangeness, there was definitely an awkwardness between us. Or maybe it was my imagination, because I seem to have far too much of it lately. Anyway, Sebastian has a full diary of meetings this morning – Jake Matinson is currently ensconced in his office with him, signing his contract and discussing his debut exhibition – so we haven't really spoken apart from to say good morning.

Clearly, sleeping tablets aren't the answer I thought they might be. Or maybe that one I took last night had gone off, because it's from Gramma's stash and will be well out of date. It's possible; I might have

just been lucky and the first one I took was still effec-
tive. But now I'm thinking it might be my apartment;
considering how well I slept at Sebastian's on the previous night, I'm wondering if it's the place that's the
problem, or the bed. Marco didn't die in my apartment, but he had been there on many occasions so
maybe I'm somehow translating that into my nightmares. Marco was in my room and in my bed; we
spent a lot of time in that bed and the fact that when
I was at Sebastian's, I slept like a log must say something, mustn't it?

Tally suddenly appears in front of my desk and
proceeds to bore me with an explanation of the con-
cept of her latest painting. Something to do with
motherhood and the modern perception of 'having it
all'. *I get it*, I want to shout, I got it after the first
couple of sentences so there's no need to go into such
tedious detail. I don't, obviously, but I do stifle a
yawn, but not quite well enough because her mouth
twists and she suddenly says she has to go and
flounces back into the gallery. Glancing at my watch,
I see that it's as near as dammit to lunchtime, so I go
out to our tiny kitchen at the back of the gallery to
have some lunch. I feel sick and have a headache; a
strong black coffee is just what I need. And I should

eat something, too, although I definitely don't feel like it.

* * *

After the coffee, I managed to get a smoothie down so that I could take some paracetamol. My headache is slowly lifting and there are only a few hours to go until home time and then it's two whole days off.

I'm hoping that Carrie will be there when I get home and tonight isn't another night where she's going to be working late; I badly need to talk to her. Also, I don't want to be alone. She's so sensible and not at all dramatic like me and will help me to see sense and get a perspective on things. A sudden noise from my desk drawer perplexes me and I pull it open and look at my mobile phone that's lying in there. The tinkling of bells is not the sound of a text or a WhatsApp and for a moment, I can't imagine what it could be. A notification banner has popped up on the screen and I stare at it blankly before I register what it is. It's the security camera over my apartment front door.

Why is this notification being sent to me when I always keep my settings turned off? I don't need to look at the footage because no one can come to our apartment without getting past security and they don't allow anyone in without checking with us first. They take in all the post and deliveries and as we're at the end of the corridor, no other residents have to pass our door.

Did I turn on notifications and forget I'd done so? This thought really bothers me far more than it should, until I remember that there was a mountain of updates due on all my apps but I hadn't updated for weeks, so I'd set it going when I saw Tally making a beeline for my desk this morning. I fiddled around with it as if I was doing something important, hoping she'd take the hint and go away. It didn't work, although the yawn did, so maybe I'll yawn loudly in her face next time. Perhaps the update turned the notifications on, so I now need to turn them off, otherwise every time Carrie or I enter or leave the house, it'll keep dinging. I threw my phone into the drawer when Tally didn't take the hint and leave, and I haven't even glanced at it since. I left it lying in the unlocked drawer whilst I was in the staff kitchen at lunchtime staring into space and trying to make sense of things. What an absolute idiot; anyone could have wandered by and helped themselves to it – as well as my handbag which is sitting underneath the desk just waiting to be stolen. I always lock everything away when I'm not at my desk; even the appointments book is put in a locked drawer because sadly, casual theft is all too common. Sebastian hates the fact that he has to have a buzzer on the door because he asserts that it puts off potential customers from coming in and browsing but that doesn't mean that once they're in here, they can't steal anything.

I've never forgotten to lock everything away or take it with me before.

Never.

I've been extremely lucky; imagine the headache of cancelling bank cards at the same time as trying to get a new phone. With a sigh, I scroll through the screens and eventually find the app and tap on the icon to change the settings. I'm about to tap out of it when I stop and think. No one should be at our door right now.

I tap on the history button and page after page of mine and Carrie's comings and goings fill the screen but at the very top is a video from mere minutes ago. Curious, I tap and open it and as it plays, my breath catches in my throat.

A man wearing a black tracksuit walks up to the apartment door, his head down, the thick, curly hair in full view of the camera as he walks.

Hair just like Marco's.

Marco's dead, Mia, it's just someone who has the same hair.

He stands for a moment looking down at his feet and then slowly turns and looks straight into the camera lens.

He smiles; the same lopsided smile that I remember from my dreams and nightmares.

It can't be.

But somehow, it is.

It's Marco.

Back from the dead.

8

I run away.

From what, I'm not sure. I just know that I can't stay in the gallery for a minute longer. I throw my phone into my bag, grab my jacket and jump up and walk as fast as I can out into the street. I keep on walking without stopping until I reach the park and finally stop at the side of the lake and stare unseeingly at the ducks bobbing up and down. I didn't stop to tell anyone I was leaving so no one will have a clue where I've gone.

I should send Sebastian a message; make an excuse as to why I've left work mid-afternoon without even bothering to tell him.

But I can't, because to do that would involve

taking my mobile phone out of my handbag and right at this moment, I can't seem to make myself do it. Which is entirely ridiculous because it's not as if the phone can hurt me.

But it feels that way; I'm afraid to touch it.

The paranoia of last night never really went away, only lessened, and I can feel it rapidly ramping up. It seems very much as if people are turning their heads to look at me as they go by. Or maybe it's not paranoia; maybe I've been standing here for too long just staring and I'm the one who looks odd. The thought makes me glance at my watch: three forty-five.

How long have I been here? I'm not sure exactly what time I left the gallery but it can't have been much after two o'clock because I hadn't been back from my lunch break for very long. What have I been doing for all that time? Just standing here, staring? No wonder people are looking at me. I step backwards from the lake and slowly make my way along the path towards a cluster of trees. There's an empty bench underneath them and I can sit there for a while and try to pull myself together. My legs feel shaky as I walk and I shiver underneath my thin blouse. This morning's forecast was for a hot day and the people walking past me are wearing summer clothing: sundresses, shorts and t-shirts;

some men have taken their shirts off, so it's definitely not cold.

Maybe it's shock.

I reach the bench, lower myself down onto it and take several deep breaths. I should have another look at the footage but the thought of seeing Marco again makes me want to curl up and die.

But I have to look. I need to prove to myself that it's not Marco. It's impossible for it to be him; he's dead and I know he's dead because I killed him. Think about it calmly, Mia; it's someone who looks like him, that's all. He looks a bit like Marco and your paranoia and panic did the rest and turned him into the man you accidentally killed.

Owen.

His name pops into my head out of nowhere and I immediately start to feel the tension leaving my body. Of course! Why didn't I think of this when I first looked at the footage; the man at the door has to be Owen. As comprehension dawns, I'm astounded by my own stupidity. I can't believe that I didn't think of Owen before I flew into a panic and ran away from the gallery as if being chased by a ghost. Owen is one of the few people who is perfectly entitled to be at my front door and is the most likely; he would have been leaving a parcel for me or for Carrie. I didn't notice the parcel because in my hysteria, I shut down the video before it had finished. Owen, Jim or whoever is on shift take in any deliveries and hand them over as we come in but occasionally, they'll leave them outside our door. I'm not expecting a delivery but Carrie must be; she does order things from Next and Amazon sometimes. Owen's most likely just trying to be nice and make up for his miserableness this morning by bringing it upstairs for us.

I begin to feel embarrassed by my own behaviour; Sebastian or someone else will surely have noticed my absence by now, so I'm going to have to think of a suitable excuse for upping and leaving. Unfortunately, I don't have any relatives that I can say have been taken ill and I rack my brains to think of an acceptable reason for deserting my post. After thinking for a while, I come up with the rather lame excuse that I spilt a full cup of coffee over myself and had to hurry home and get changed. I'm hoping that Sebastian won't notice that I'm still wearing the clothes I arrived in this morning; he shouldn't, because men are completely unobservant about things like that. I'll write the text as if I've just left and act surprised that he only received it just before I get back. I'll blame the network or something.

I pull out my phone and hover over the apps before pressing firmly on the front-door camera. Time to put a stop to this nonsense; just look at the screen and confirm it's Owen and get on with your life, Mia. I click on the app, open up the history and without pausing, click straight onto the most recent video. I watch the dark-clothed figure approach the front door carefully to see if he has a parcel in his arms but am unable to see the other side of him, so the box must be quite small. As he slowly raises his head towards the camera, I peer closer, intent on satisfying myself that it's Owen.

But it's not. It's Marco. Without a doubt. I freeze the screen and study it with mounting horror before closing the app and dropping the phone into my handbag as if it's burning my fingers.

I stand up and hook my handbag over my shoulder. I can't stay here any longer.

I need a drink.

* * *

The bar is starting to fill up with Friday-night revellers who've come straight from work to kickstart their weekend with plenty of alcohol. They congregate around the bar ordering their drinks before spilling onto the surrounding tables. It won't be long before they reach my table and people will want to sit in the empty seats. I'll be surrounded. I need to get up and leave before that happens and I'm forced to fight my way through hordes of people.

As I look around, I envy them with their loud voices and laughter because they don't have a care in the world and all they have to worry about is who's buying the next drink.

That was me not so long ago.

Before I ruined my life in one idiotic moment.

I lean over the table and push the empty wine bottle further away from me in an attempt to make it less obvious that I've drunk the whole lot myself. Too late, I realise that I should have asked for two wine glasses and pretended that someone else was with me. I drain the last drop of wine from the glass and wonder what I'm going to do now. I may have drunk a whole bottle of wine but I don't feel any better for it: not even drunk.

I just feel sick.

I open my bag and peer down at my phone: still no reply from Carrie. I've sent her three messages and she hasn't read any of them. It's well after six o'clock now, so surely she'll be finishing work soon. Shamefully, although I know she's a chartered accountant, I have only a vague idea of what she actually does. The very minute the words *financial services* are uttered, my brain switches off with the certainly that whatever follows will be boring beyond belief.

I haven't looked at the video again; I don't need to because every second of it is imprinted on my brain. The sensible part of me knows that I should open the app and screenshot it to send to Carrie.

But I can't bring myself to; I'm too afraid to see Marco's face again and confirm that he's back from the dead.

I'm a pathetic coward.

The hope that I'm clinging onto is that Carrie will know what to do; Carrie always knows what to do.

'Anyone sitting here?'

A greyed-suited city boy with a sharp haircut is standing in front of me. He has his head to one side with a cocky grin on his face and a bottle of beer in each hand.

'No,' I say, shaking my head.

I need to leave. Now. The clamour in the bar is getting louder by the minute, loud, braying voices, whooping noises and hoots of laughter. Why are some people so obnoxious the minute they've had so much as a sip of alcohol?

My arm jolts and I realise grey-suit has dropped

into the seat next to me, knocking my arm in the process.

'Oops, sorry. Clumsy me.' He grins at me, showing very white teeth which I can't seem to take my eyes off.

'What's someone as lovely as you doing all on their lonesome?'

Oh God, he's making a pass at me.

I stand up, or I attempt to, but something seems to have happened to my legs. I've been sitting here for too long.

'One too many, eh? Or not enough? Here, have this.'

He thrusts one of the bottles of beer towards me. I look at it for a moment and for some reason, take it from him even though my head is screaming, *NO*.

'I'm Charlie, nice to meet you.' He puts his hand out to me and after a moment, I take it.

'Mia.'

His fingers wrap around mine and he holds my hand for a moment too long. I jerk my hand away when he starts to stroke my thumb.

He grins at me again and out of nowhere, I have the overpowering urge to punch his smug face. Rage bubbles up inside me and the sound of voices and laughter takes on a nightmarish quality. I've had this feeling before and it never ends well. I stand up abruptly and pick up my bag, but I can't get out; his chair is in my way.

'Excuse me.' It sounds as if my voice is coming from a very long way away.

'Not leaving, are you?' The grin has gone now, replaced by a frown, giving his face a ratty look. 'After I bought you a drink, as well.'

I want to tell him that he never bought it for me, but I don't trust myself to speak. The rage is building and without answering, I try to squeeze past him. He folds his arms and refuses to move and the grin returns.

'You've got to pay if you want to get by; a little kiss for Charlie should do it. No tongues, I promise.'

I stare down at his grinning face for a moment before leaning down until my mouth is next to his ear. I see his grin grow wider as I move closer.

'Get out of my way,' I hiss into his ear. 'Or else I'll fucking knife you.'

* * *

I'm walking away from the pub. Fast.

I don't even have a knife.

He moved out of my way though, quickly, and as I walked away, he muttered, 'Fucking psycho bitch.'

I vomit when I'm halfway down the street; it starts with a hiccup and I taste the sourness of the wine and before I know it, I've stumbled into a shop doorway and am throwing up like a common drunk. It spews from my mouth in a foul-smelling fountain and I wonder how there can be so much of it. I stagger out of the doorway afterwards wiping my mouth and when I see the stares of disgust from passers-by, I feel ashamed at how low I've sunk.

I continue walking. I can't seem to walk in a straight line and I can't understand how I can still feel so drunk when I must surely have expelled every drop of wine from my body. As I walk, I realise that I'm heading towards home.

Towards Marco.

What if he's there, waiting for me?

I stop in my tracks and try to think through the fog in my brain.

Where else can I go?

There is nowhere else.

I'll go home but I won't go in; I'll wait outside and when I get there, I'll message Carrie to see where she is. If she's inside, it'll be safe.

Unless he's waiting for Carrie, too.

I push the thought away. I can't think about that at the moment because if I do, the hysteria starts to rise. Calm down. It'll take me about an hour to get home and the walk will sober me up. It will stop my mind from wandering back to the video. I begin to walk and although I've walked this route many times, I've never done it in this stumbling, zigzagging fashion. Usually, it's a pleasant amble on a sunny day. I briefly consider calling a cab but decide not to, fearful that the stench of vomit will be apparent as soon as I get inside the car. I don't look at my phone to see if Carrie has replied because it doesn't matter; for now, I need to keep walking. I just need to get home and get inside and away from everyone.

As long as Carrie is there and Marco isn't.

The walk helps; by the time I reach the apartment block, I feel less agitated and more in control. Maybe throwing up wasn't such a bad thing because I'm feeling almost sober; perhaps I was more drunk than I realised.

I pull my phone out of my bag to see that Carrie has replied to my messages:

I'm at home. What's wrong?? xx

I look at the three messages I've sent her; they all say the same thing:

Where are you???

I slip my phone in my pocket, open the door and walk into the foyer. An unfamiliar face is sitting at the security desk and I'm grateful for his anonymity because I don't want to be seen in this state. He's one of the agency casuals and I feel thankful that I don't feel obliged to stop and make small talk. What if he smelt the vomit on me? How humiliating that would be. I wave and call out a brief hello, without stopping, and continue straight into the lift which, mercifully, is standing vacant with the doors open.

When the lift stops at our floor, I step outside and walk down the corridor to the apartment. The front door is pulled open before I even have to knock or use my key and Carrie is standing in front of me.

'Mia! What's happened? I've been so worried.'

'You're alone?' I ask, my voice hoarse.

'Of course I'm alone, who else would be here?' She laughs.

The relief is immense. She's okay. He's not there.

'I don't know,' I say as I stumble inside and she closes the door behind me.

She gives me a strange look before guiding me into the lounge, where I flop onto the sofa, kick my shoes off and throw my handbag onto the floor, exhaustion hitting me like a physical force.

'Have you been drinking?'

'A bit.'

I lay my head against the sofa and close my eyes. I'm so tired. So, so tired. My brain slows and begins to drift; I feel safe for the first time in hours. I want to sleep.

'Mia?'

I reluctantly open my eyes. Carrie is staring at me with concern.

'Are you okay?'

'No. Yes – I am now you're here.'

'What's happened? I've been ringing you for the last half an hour, why didn't you answer? Have you lost your phone?'

I shake my head and look around before reaching down and pulling my handbag towards me. I rummage around inside it and eventually find my phone. I take it out. I look at the screen to see there are several missed calls from Carrie. 'Why didn't I hear or see them? I looked at my phone mere minutes ago to read your messages.'

'I don't know. Maybe you turned the sound down.'

Did I? I don't remember doing it, but maybe I did.

'Has something happened?' Carrie looks worried and I nod.

'The video thing. Marco is on there.'

'What?'

'The front door camera on my phone. The app. I got a notification this afternoon to say someone was on it. It's Marco, at the door. He's come back.'

'That's not possible, Mia, you know that. He can't come back,' she says slowly.

'I know it's not possible, it shouldn't be possible, but he's on there, Carrie. Look at the video and you'll see.' She picks up her phone from the coffee table and sits down next to me. I stare ahead, unwilling to see Marco's face again.

'What's the app called?'

'ALC. It's the bright-blue button.'

We sit in silence as she scrolls through her phone and I close my eyes as if that will make it all go away. How can Marco be alive? How? He can't; his ghost has come back for revenge. He's going to haunt me and scare me to death. People die of fright. They do.

'Mia?' Carrie's voice has a wobble to it and I can

tell without even looking at her that she's as shaken as I am.

'It's him, isn't it?' My voice sounds hollow, as if there's nothing left in me; the person sitting here a mere shell of the old Mia.

There's silence for a moment, before Carrie answers.

'I can't see anyone, Mia. The only videos on here are of you and me.'

My eyes fly open and I stare at her as she holds the screen in front of me.

'See. Just you and me, no one else.'

I take the phone from her and scroll through the videos. I stare at the screen. She's right; the video isn't on there.

No Marco.

'He's on mine.' I pick up my phone from my lap. 'Maybe yours hasn't updated properly or something. He's on here, look.'

I open the app and scroll to the videos, holding the screen so that we can both see it. I brace myself for the sight of Marco's face again, scrolling past the videos of me and Carrie arriving home and then further on and then back again, frantically trying to find it. I've missed it.

Slow down. Calm down.

I go through each video slowly, right back to the beginning of the week. I find video after video of me and Carrie.

But not one of Marco.

He's not there.

The video has gone.

9

'I saw him,' I insist. 'I saw him.'

Carrie doesn't speak but gently takes my phone from my hands and places it on the table next to hers.

'I don't understand. It was there, Carrie, it was there. Marco was here outside our door as plain as day. I'm not lying. He smiled straight into the camera.'

'I know you're not lying, Mia, of course you're not. Did you take a screenshot of what you saw?'

I shake my head. I didn't because I was a coward and didn't want to look at him. How stupid I am, how gutless. I had proof and I've lost it because I'm weak. I stare at my phone as if I can will the footage to reappear. I don't understand it.

'Maybe I deleted it by accident when I looked at it the last time.' I'd drunk an entire bottle of wine; I might have thought I was sober and knew what I was doing but I obviously didn't. I threatened to knife a man, didn't I? Hardly the actions of a sober, rational person. Because of my stupid drunken state, I've managed to wipe the only evidence there is that Marco is still alive. Because he must be alive; there is no such thing as ghosts. Somehow, he survived and escaped. The people who were supposed to dispose of his body have lied.

And he's coming to get me; that much is obvious. He wants revenge.

'He was on there, Carrie. Alive and well and smiling straight into the lens as if he was staring right into my soul. He's here and he's going to get me. It's just a matter of time.'

'He's not, Mia; he's dead,' Carrie says quietly. 'We both know that. You know that because you shot him through the heart and no one can survive that.'

I shake my head.

'No. He's not dead. I've seen him. Somehow – I don't know how – he's survived. He might have looked dead but he wasn't. He's tricked us.'

The words hang in the air and I try to remember the moments after I pulled the trigger. The strange smell that reminded me of fireworks, the way he lay there, not moving. I never went over to him, so could he have been alive? He could have been unconscious and Carrie thought he was dead but he was really only injured. The bullet could have gone into his chest and missed his heart; it's possible.

'If he'd been here, he'd be on my phone too, wouldn't he?' Carrie says gently. 'And he's not, because he's dead.'

'No. He's alive. I know it. Somehow, they've deleted the footage. That's easy to do nowadays, isn't it? They can deepfake people's faces and stuff, so deleting a video is easy. A kid could probably do it.'

'From both our phones?'

'Yes! Anything is possible now. Anything. They could have done it remotely. He's alive, I know it.'

'But why would they delete it, and who are "they"?' Carrie asks.

'I don't know.' I hold my head in my hands. Think, Mia, *think*. The answer is there if I can just think clearly and find it.

'He's dead, Mia. Dead. He's been disposed of,' Carrie bursts out suddenly. 'I didn't want to tell you any of the details but it's impossible for him to be alive because he's buried in many different places.'

'Different places?' I echo, as the reality of what she's saying sinks in. She means they chopped him up. I gasp at the horror of it as well as the picture it conjures up, and clamp my hand over my mouth.

'I'm sorry, Mia; I didn't want to have to tell you, but you have to understand that it's not possible for him to be alive. That's what they do, these people from my past, people you don't ever want to meet; they're from the dark web, from the other side of life that normal people don't even know exists. They make sure a body is never found. Never. Mostly, time and wild animals destroy any evidence that's left and the body parts are never found but if they are, they're so decomposed that they're untraceable. I know you believe you saw him, but the truth is, Marco is dead and he's never coming back. He can't come back.'

I shake my head, refusing to believe what she's saying although I so badly want to. If only I hadn't been so drunk. I'm so stupid: so, so stupid.

'You've been under so much strain.' Carrie puts her arm around me. 'You're struggling to cope with the guilt of killing him. With the nightmares you've been having, you've hardly slept for weeks and that's taken its toll.'

I look up at her, her words sinking in. 'You think I imagined it? Him?'

Carries hesitates for a moment before answering. 'No. Yes. Maybe... The mind can play funny tricks on you. You said yourself that you've not been feeling right.'

Did I imagine it?

I didn't, I'm sure I didn't.

'It was so real. He stared right at me and he smiled. Just the way he used to; that same cocky smile that said he could do whatever he liked to me and I would go along with it.'

Carrie pulls me to her, wraps her arms around me and holds me tightly. After a moment, I give in and relax and as I do so, I feel the rigidity and tension of the last hours begin to leave me. Carrie must be right; I couldn't have seen Marco, could I?

He's dead and I know that because I killed him.

* * *

'Hi Owen.' I have my most winning smile on my face even though inside, I feel sick. I was hoping that Jim would be on shift; despite him being more formal and reticent, I don't feel awkward with him like I do now with Owen.

He looks up from the desk where he has some sort of form spread out in front of him. I know he's already seen me because he glanced up as the lift doors opened.

'Morning, Miss Enderby.'

The words are spoken pleasantly enough but he's not smiling at all which is not a good sign. I wonder why I ever thought him childlike and puppyish; the Owen who was so eager to please me and desperate for my attention seems like a completely different person to the man in front of me.

'I was wondering Owen, if I might see yesterday morning's CCTV footage of the entrance doors into the building?'

'CCTV?' Owen raises one eyebrow and I realise he's not going to make this easy for me.

'Yes please. My door camera picked up someone leaving a parcel for me but the box is damaged so I need to check who it was that delivered it. The delivery company asked me to get a description of them as they have several drivers in this area and couldn't pinpoint which one it might be.'

It's a lame excuse but was the best I could come up with, especially after a night of no sleep. No nightmares last night but that's not surprising considering that I didn't even go to sleep because I was in absolute turmoil.

Did I imagine seeing Marco? I have to accept that I did because, as Carrie told me, we were both there when he died. The evidence – that I was so convinced I had – never existed. I can pretend to myself that I accidentally deleted it, but the truth is that it was never there in the first place, which explains why it wasn't on Carrie's phone, either. Seeing Marco wherever I go, and the feelings of being watched that I've been having, are obviously all in my mind.

Knowing what I did to Marco has made me paranoid.

And yet even though I've told Carrie that I accept I must have imagined it, I have to prove this to myself, somehow. If I can see the CCTV footage from yesterday morning, it will show that I imagined the whole thing because Marco won't be on there. My brain needs to see this and then I can accept that all of the times I've thought I saw Marco, it was my overactive imagination. I've waited until Carrie had gone to the gym before coming down here because I don't want her to worry that I still believe he's alive. I've accepted that my mind is playing tricks on me.

I just need to be sure.

All I have to do is view it and then I'll be able to ra-
tionalise it the next time my brain tries to convince me
that Marco is still alive. The logical part of me is fully
aware that he's dead and if I had any doubts at all,
Carrie was a witness. I need to see the footage for myself
so I can move on and get some help, although how I can
do that without telling anyone the truth, I don't know.
For now, I need to see the footage and put an end to it.

Because there is a small part of me that thinks I
really did see Marco and whilst I still have that tiny
doubt, I'm never going to be able to move forward
without confirming that it wasn't him with my own
eyes.

I've had to apply make-up to cover the dark circles underneath my eyes and although I'm so tired I
could probably fall asleep standing up, the thought
of the resulting nightmare if I did is enough to keep
me awake.

'I was on the desk yesterday morning. We don't
let delivery drivers come in and drop parcels off at
your door. We keep them here for you or take them
upstairs ourselves.'

'Maybe they popped in when you were otherwise
engaged and took it upstairs?' I suggest.

I mean when he went to the toilet; he must have
to go at some point, mustn't he? There's a door be-

hind the security desk that leads into a little office so I'm guessing they have a toilet in there. No one can go for twelve hours without using the toilet.

Owen shakes his head. 'No one can come in without the door code so if there's no one at the desk, they'd have to wait for us to let them in. It's impossible for a delivery driver to take anything up to your apartment without us knowing.'

He's speaking like a robot and I begin to feel irritated by him; *just let me see the CCTV, Owen, and I'll go away. Stop being such an arse.* Besides which, the paranoid side of my brain tells me, Marco knew the code to get in, so he could easily come and go as he pleased. In fact, God knows who else has the code because it hasn't changed in all the years I've lived here.

'Can I see it anyway?'

'Please,' I add when he doesn't reply.

'I'm sorry, Miss Enderby, but under company policy we're not allowed to show the footage to anyone except security personnel.' He doesn't sound sorry; he sounds pleased.

'But I live here, surely I've got a right to see who's coming and going?'

He smiles slightly. 'I'm not allowed to show you, but if you really need to see it, you can write to head office for permission. They're the only ones who can permit it. I can give you the address if you like.'

I stare down at him, fully aware that he's enjoying every moment of this conversation.

'Give me the address,' I snap. 'Better still, give me their email address and I'll do it immediately. This is ridiculous.'

Owen shuffles some paper around before producing a business card from a plastic box next to the telephone and handing it to me. I take it from him and study it.

'There's no email address on there,' I state.

He shrugs very slightly and I push down the mounting anger that I feel towards him. I should have waited until Jim or one of the casuals was on shift but I want to see it now; I don't want to wait.

'They'll reply by post within twenty-eight days. We keep the CCTV recordings for ninety days, so it won't be a problem.'

Without another word, I turn and stalk furiously back towards the lift. I'll wait until Owen's gone off shift and try again with one of the others although I'm not optimistic. If it is against company policy, then they won't allow it either. That's if Owen is telling the truth; I wouldn't be surprised if he's lying because he now seems to have it in for me. If it is

company policy, do I really want to write to head office and make myself look ridiculous with my beyond
lame reason for asking to see it?

I can't wait twenty-eight days, I just can't; I need to
see it now so I can tell my brain to shut up. Maybe I
am going mad. Maybe I'm already mad and I don't
realise it yet. Do mad people know that they're mad?
I don't think they do.

I stab the button to summon the lift and stand
and seethe. I turn and look over to see Owen staring
at me and making no attempt to hide the fact that
he's doing so.

He's glaring at me as if he hates me.

We continue to stare at each other but even when
the lift arrives and I hear the doors open, I don't
move.

Enough.

I'm going to get it out in the open and put an end
to this; I'll apologise for being rude to him if that'll
do the trick, although, actually, I wasn't rude, not really. He's not a friend of mine, he's a security guard
who works in the building where I own a very expensive apartment. I pay an extortionate management
fee every month which pays his wages. Maybe I won't
apologise; maybe I'll ask him why he's being so
bloody rude and unhelpful. I spin around on my heel

and march towards him. He continues to hold my gaze without wavering.

I'm the one who looks away first.

'Owen,' I say, as I arrive at his desk. 'There's something I need to say.'

He looks down and slowly folds the piece of paper in front of him into two and then places it carefully to one side.

He looks up and smiles at me, his eyes cold.

'There's nothing to say.' The smile vanishes. 'I know what you did, Mia. I know.'

10

I open my eyes and for a moment I have no idea where I am. The panic begins to rise before I remember that I'm at Sebastian's flat. I relax and snuggle down under the duvet and then wonder where he is because the space next to me is empty. There's no doubt that I feel better here; my head feels clearer and I'm less paranoid, more in control. I've come to the conclusion that I'll have to move from my apartment to somewhere different, buy a new place or maybe upsize to a house. I have the money and it's just sitting there earning interest when it would earn much more invested in bricks and mortar. I should have invested it in another property when I first gained access to my trust fund when I was twenty-one, because the value of the property would have increased massively by now. The apartment was my first home on my own but it's about time I moved elsewhere.

Get away from the bad memories.

And Owen.

I could keep the flat and rent it out, use it as a monthly income and while I'm doing that it'll be going up in value. It's something to think about and perhaps I'll make a few enquiries at an estate agent this week; get the ball rolling, as they say. The thought of it cheers me up; I'm taking positive action to get my life back to normal and expunge the spectre of Marco from my life.

The bedroom door is open and I'm sure I can smell the aroma of coffee wafting into the room; maybe Sebastian is making us breakfast in bed. I pull myself up, plump up the pillows and rake my fingers through my hair to fluff it up a bit. Have I got time to pop to the bathroom and brush my teeth to get rid of the morning breath? I don't want to get caught doing that so probably not; I'll just wait and gulp some coffee, when he brings it.

Coming here yesterday was a spur of the moment thing; Sebastian and I hadn't arranged to see each other over the weekend but I knew that I couldn't stay in my apartment alone for a minute longer. Carrie's working hours are too erratic to rely on her for company and the thought of rattling around on my own was too much to bear.

Too much time for thinking; too much time for my overactive brain to make things up and scare me half to death.

After Owen told me that he knew, I stared at him in horror and then turned and ran straight for the lift and went back upstairs. I was in a blind panic and so many thoughts were whirling through my head that I just had to get away so I could think. But the minute I was back inside the flat, I felt the walls closing in; Owen knew.

He knew.

How could he? No one knows except for me and Carrie. No one. And then I remembered: the dark web. The people who cleared up the aftermath, disposed of Marco's body; they knew. How many people were involved? Is Owen part of the dark web? What if he was involved in it? I told myself I was being ridiculous, but it didn't work; this wasn't my imagination any more, Owen has changed towards me and it's because he's found out what I did, not because I was rude to him. He's going to blackmail me, I'm sure, and who knows what else he might make me do?

When this dawned on me, I ran out into the hallway, bolted the front door and rang Sebastian to see if I could stay at his.

I could have gone to Suki's or one of my other friends but to be honest, I didn't know what reason I could give for turning up on their doorstep and asking to stay when I had a perfectly good apartment of my own. Sebastian was easier; I was seeing him, we're almost in a relationship, so there would be no awkward questions asked. I hoped. I calmed myself down and rang him, surprising myself with how normal I sounded. He couldn't hide his surprise when he answered and was then very offhand with me and I couldn't understand why until he asked me where the hell I'd disappeared to on Friday after-noon without telling him.

With everything that had happened, I'd forgotten how I'd left work without a word to anyone. I remem-bered then that I never did send a message to tell him where I'd gone so he would have had no idea where I was or why I'd suddenly vanished. I instantly de-cided that the spilt coffee excuse wasn't going to wash with him, so I lied massively and told him the only thing that I thought could possibly excuse my be-haviour.

A death in the family.

Not mine, obviously, because I don't have any relatives. I told him that Carrie had rung me in a panic because she'd been informed that one of her close family members had been in a horrific car accident and died. She was near hysterical, I told him, and was already at home in the apartment so I made the instant decision to get home as quickly as possible to comfort her.

I think he believed me.

He thawed a bit after that because he couldn't actually call me a liar, could he? Obviously, I grovelled like mad and said how sorry I was that I'd run off in such a panic and then I offered to take him out for dinner to make it up to him. He readily agreed and that's when I began to think that maybe he really likes me. I think he does, probably more than I like him, which is often the way it goes with normal, well brought up guys like Sebastian. I asked if I should bring my overnight bag with me and he seemed pleased about that.

So here I am: yesterday morning and Owen are now just a bad memory that has an unreal quality about it. I didn't quite know how I was going to bring myself to walk past Owen but as luck would have it, an elderly neighbour from one of the other apartments was getting into the lift as I locked the front door and she held the lift and waited for me. I made sure to engage her in conversation and when we stepped out of the lift into the foyer, I never even glanced over at Owen but kept talking to her as we walked out onto the street.

I'm sure I could feel him looking at me, though.

I just have to keep out of his way and not give him any opportunity to speak to me. He's not on shift all of the time, thankfully. I haven't told Carrie what he said to me because it's not the sort of thing you can put in a message, is it? I'll tell her when I see her and she'll have to do something, get whoever's in charge to tell Owen to leave me alone. Because I paid to make it all go away, for God's sake.

'Breakfast is served, madam.' Sebastian is standing in the bedroom doorway in just his boxer shorts, holding a tray with coffee, orange juice and croissants on it.

'I wondered where you'd got to.'

He brings the tray over and places it on the bedside table and climbs in next to me.

'This is nice.' I smile up at him. He reaches across and picks up a cup and offers it to me.

'Thought we could have breakfast and then go for a walk on the Heath and grab lunch somewhere nice, what do you think?'

I take the coffee from him and take a sip.

'Sounds perfect.'

Sebastian smiles and kisses me on the nose and I get a blast of minty breath; he's cleaned his teeth already. He stares into my eyes with a serious expression on his face and I giggle.

'Don't laugh at me.' There's a hint of anger in his voice.

'I'm not laughing at you, I'm just happy.'

'Really?' He frowns. 'Because I was starting to think that you'd gone off me after your disappearing act.'

'I did explain.'

'I know. But I can't help feeling hurt that you didn't even think to come and tell me what had happened. I could have helped, you know.' He looks upset and I feel bad.

'I'm so sorry. I was in such a panic and Carrie was in absolute pieces on the phone. I'm just a thoughtless idiot who simply doesn't think. Can you ever forgive me?'

'Of course.' He studies my face. 'Although you're lucky I'm more than just your boss otherwise you'd have some explaining to do.'

He's letting me know, of course, that I'm an employee and running away from my post is not acceptable. I feel slightly annoyed that he has to say it and maybe this shows in my face because he gently brushes a strand of hair out of my eyes and smiles.

'I was worried. I had no idea where you were, and I thought something had happened to you; one minute you were there and the next you were gone. Luckily, Tally told me she saw you dashing out of the gallery otherwise I might have contacted the police. You never answered any of my calls; it was as if you'd vanished off the face of the earth. I was concerned, Mia, and it made me realise how much I care about you.' He sighs and we lock eyes. 'I had a sleepless night last night, thinking about you, thinking that you'd gone off me.'

'Oh, Sebastian, I'm so sorry. Of course I haven't gone off you.'

'Good to hear.' He smiles. 'Very good to hear.' He leans close and we kiss. 'Just don't run off like that again, yeah?'

Wow. He must really like me.

* * *

I stride rapidly through the foyer without turning my head, determined not to even glance in Owen's direction. I know he's sitting behind the desk because I saw the back of him through the window but I refuse to look. I step into the lift and press the button, sighing with relief when the doors close before he has a chance to get up from his desk.

I let myself into the flat and lock and bolt the door. I know that Carrie is already home because I messaged her to find out where she was before I left Sebastian's. We had a lovely late lunch in a tiny bistro that we found and I think Sebastian would have quite liked me to stay over again. Although I was tempted, I told him I needed more clothes and would see him tomorrow.

I think I'll be spending a lot more time at Sebastian's from now on though, at least until I get myself somewhere new to live.

'Why have you bolted the door?' Carrie is standing in the lounge doorway, looking at me with a puzzled expression.

'We have a problem, Carrie, a big one.'

'A problem? What sort of problem?'

'Owen,' I say.

'Owen? Why would he be a problem?' She smiles. 'Has he been making puppy-dog eyes at you again?'

'No. He knows.'

'Knows what?'

'About Marco.'

She laughs. 'Of course he doesn't know, that's not possible. Whatever makes you think he knows?'

I tell her then, about wanting to see the CCTV, which I didn't really want to admit to. I impress on her that it was only to fully convince myself that I'd imagined seeing Marco. When I tell her what Owen says, she looks shocked.

'He actually said those exact words? "I know what you did"?'

'Yes.'

'Shit.' She looks thoughtful and I wait for her to tell me what she's going to do about it.

I hope there's something she can do.

'Okay,' Carrie says after a while. 'I can get a message to the guy, the one who arranged everything. He'll sort it out because they won't like it. What Owen's said makes them look bad. Untrustworthy. Everything they do is about trust. Just avoid Owen, okay? Don't get into conversation with him at all, don't speak to him. If he tries to talk to you, keep walking and don't engage.'

'Okay.'

'And don't worry, everything will be fine. This is just a blip. I'll message my contact and it'll go up the chain and once they know, they'll put a stop to Owen.'

'You're sure?'

Carrie laughs grimly. 'Quite sure. These people are not to be messed with.'

The thought crosses my mind that Owen could find himself in trouble. He's buried in many different places sort of trouble. They'll put a stop to Owen. That doesn't sound good, and I shudder at what might happen to him and experience a pang of regret. I don't want anything bad to happen to him. I remind myself it's not my fault; Owen shouldn't have tried to blackmail me or whatever it is he intends on doing.

Carrie takes out her phone and goes into the lounge and I try not to think about what they might do to him. I pick up my overnight bag and take it into the bedroom and unpack, tossing everything into the laundry basket. I don't relish the thought of sleeping here tonight and I make a mental note to ring an estate agent first thing tomorrow morning and start looking for somewhere else to live. I haven't told Carrie about my plan but once I've found a house, I will. There'll be plenty of room in my new place so she can still live with me; I don't think I'll move too far from here.

My phone pings and I pick it up from the bed to

see a new text message. It's from an unknown number.

Delete it, Mia, just delete it.

But I can't; I have to see what it says.

I click on it with a sense of foreboding and read the words in front of me.

I know what you did and you'll be sorry.

11

I scroll through my emails and congratulate myself on taking the first step in my search for a new place to live. I contacted an estate agent first thing this morning and asked them to send me any properties in this area of London that meet my criteria. They're super-keen because I've already received three properties from them. I've also set up an alert on a massive online property search engine for specific properties and I have a bunch of emailed property details to look through.

I'm on my lunch break, sitting in the staff kitchen sifting through them as I sip my smoothie, and I've already earmarked two that might be suitable. I feel a tingle of excitement at the thought of a new house – possibly with a garden – and decide that it'll be fun furnishing and decorating a new home. Not that I'll be doing any actual painting or anything but I'll enjoy choosing the colours. Maybe I'll get an interior designer in to make sure it's right on trend.

My phone chirrups with a new text message and I have a moment of unease, imagining it to be another threatening message. After my initial ridiculous notion that Marco was sending messages from hell, I realised that it had to be from Owen. On Carrie's advice, I blocked the number immediately and I remind myself of this as I tap and open it. It's from the estate agent asking me if any of the properties they've sent me are suitable. They're eager but they can wait; I have no intention of being hurried as I want to take my time to find exactly the right house.

I managed to sleep last night which is pretty amazing considering all that's happened these last few days. I did wake in the early hours with the thought of Owen on my mind but, surprisingly, I didn't feel overly bad because I knew it was all under control. I'm finally getting some perspective on it all. Carrie heard from her contact last night and assured me that there'll be no more veiled threats from Owen and I took her at her word and didn't torment myself imagining all sorts. It's nothing to do with me. When I got up this morning, in the spirit of my new positive attitude, I told Carrie I was looking for somewhere else to live, making sure that she knew she'd always have a home with me. She was a little surprised and asked if I wasn't being a bit hasty but as I said to her, much better to invest my inheritance into property than leave it lying around in savings accounts when interest rates aren't exactly high. The more we talked about it, the more I realised that I should really have done it a long time ago instead of being lazy and leaving it all to my accountant and solicitor. This whole Marco thing has made me realise that it's time I grew up. 'Who knows?' I said to Carrie. 'I may even start behaving like a grown-up and open my post instead of stuffing it unopened into a drawer.'

But not yet: not too many changes at once. Besides, it's all so tedious and boring.

My positive mood wasn't even spoilt by having to see Owen because he wasn't in the foyer when I left this morning; Jim was sitting at the desk and I've never been so pleased to see him. I think he was quite taken aback with my beaming smile and loud good morning as I strolled by. Knowing that he'll still be on shift when I get home makes me feel a little easier about coming back.

Lunchtime nearly over, I delete the emails of houses I'm not interested in and keep the rest to have a good look at when I get home. I can show them to Carrie and get her opinion on them. I tuck my phone into my pocket and go through the gallery and back to my desk on reception. I've just settled into my seat when Sebastian breezes through the door. He winks at me as he gets closer, looks around to make sure no one is about and plonks himself on the edge of the desk, leans over and gives me a lingering kiss on the lips.

'Hmm.' He smacks his lips together. 'Interesting flavour. What have you been eating?'

'Spinach, cucumber and avocado smoothie.'

He pulls a face. 'Yuk, that's disgusting. I wish I hadn't asked. I've just been treated to a very rare steak at Gino's, courtesy of Natasha. She's trying to persuade me to give the gallery a makeover.'

Natasha is an interior designer, brilliant – but very expensive. Maybe she could do my new house.

'And now I need caffeine.' Sebastian stands up. 'Natasha may be an excellent interior designer but hours of talking about colours and themes is enough to send anyone into a coma. Do you want one?'

'Yes please.'

Sebastian heads towards the kitchen and I check

my phone again to make sure I don't have any more emails from the estate agents. I don't. I slip the phone into my drawer and close it, then lock it and slip the key in my pocket.

Sebastian soon reappears with two mugs of coffee and is about to make himself comfortable on the corner of my desk again when I remind him that he has a Zoom call in ten minutes. He rolls his eyes before depositing one mug on my desk and heading down the corridor to his office. I wonder how much longer we can keep our relationship secret at work. It's really only the other artists and Trina and Debby, our part-time ladies and of course, the ever-present Tally, who might notice, but do we have to announce it? It's actually no one else's business. I'll leave it to Sebastian; he's the boss, let him make the decision. I drink my coffee whilst I make a few telephone calls to try and muster up a bit of interest in Jake's forthcoming exhibition. I succeed in gaining five definite attendees and two possibles to add to the twenty-five I already have. I confirm the attendees by email and then think what to do next. I click on mine and Sebastian's diaries and update them and sit back and look around. I'm bored. I look at my watch to see that it's only five past three and somehow, I have nothing left to do for the rest of the day unless a customer comes in and wants a guided tour. Sebastian is still on his Zoom call and being a Monday-afternoon dead zone, customers are few and far between.

I get up and go back to the kitchen and wash up my mug and then come back out and have a wander around. I check the various rooms to make sure they're tidy, as customers aren't immune to leaving discarded wrappers or old newspapers lying round as if we're their personal dustbin men. We don't allow food in the gallery for obvious reasons but on one occasion, I found the boxes from a McDonalds meal underneath one of the chairs in the room at the back, complete with melted half-full McFlurry container. Some of Tally's paintings have been moved from the main gallery to the smaller rooms to make way for Jake's and she's not happy about it. As Sebastian explained to her, we only have a limited amount of wall space and it has to be shared. She likes to be the centre of attention and can't stand it that Jake's debut exhibition next week will mean more of her paintings will be moved to make way for his.

I stand in front of Jake's largest picture and study it. To me, it looks like a giraffe but the title of it is *Media in Motion* so I don't think it can be.

'Looks like some sort of animal,' a voice says from

behind me. I turn around to see Tally standing there with a smirk.

'Do you think so?' I ask, trying not to laugh.

'Ya. Absolutely. All those yellow and brown stripey brush strokes put me in mind of a giraffe.'

I can't help it, I burst out laughing and then immediately regret it; it's totally inappropriate to laugh at an artist's work, especially in front of a competing artist. I'm surprised at myself.

'You are funny, Tally,' I say, pretending I'm laughing at what she's said, not the painting.

'Am I?' she asks, studying me for a moment, head on one side.

'You are. The stripes denote news and the yellow patches are how we receive good news.'

'If you say so.'

I feel a trickle of sweat run down my back and I wonder how it's become so warm in here. We have air-conditioning to protect the paintings and it shouldn't be this hot. Too much heat isn't good for paint and mixed media. Maybe the air-con has broken down. I'll have to speak to Trina or Debby about it.

'Do you think it's a bit hot in here, Tally?'

She wraps her long, woolly cardigan around herself and hugs her arms to her body. 'You're joking. It's absolutely freezing, I could almost put my coat on. Bloody air-con.'

I laugh and Tally stares at me.

'Are you okay, Mia?'

'Of course I'm okay,' I say with another laugh. 'Why wouldn't I be?'

'Dunno.' She shrugs. 'You just seem a bit, y'know, manic.'

* * *

This afternoon dragged on and seemed like forever. I had to stop looking at my watch because it seemed as if the hands barely moved and time had stopped. I've opted to take the long walk home because I've been so bored, I need to release the pent-up energy from doing nothing for the last two hours.

Maybe I should get a new job as well as a new house; if Sebastian and I are going to have a proper relationship, people are going to find out and I'm going to feel uncomfortable working there. And if we don't have a relationship, well, I'll have to leave anyway. Perhaps it's time to actually get myself a career instead of drifting around doing not very much. This thought is in my mind as I reach the apartment building and as I punch in the code to get in, I stare through the window to see the back of Owen's head. My heart sinks.

What the hell is he doing here?

I stride through the doors and despite my resolve not to look, I glance over at the desk to see that it's not Owen at all, but a stranger with dark hair talking to Jim.

Now that I look at him properly, he's nothing like Owen at all; he's short, stocky and about fifty years old and the only resemblance to Owen is dark hair, although it's straight, not curly.

'Evening Miss Enderby.' Jim nods at me and somehow, I find that I've walked over to the desk and am standing feet away from the stranger. He's wearing the same uniform as Jim.

'Just showing Robert around. He's going to be starting full-time next week on the alternate shift to me. Robert, this is Miss Enderby, apartment twenty-five.'

Robert gives me a tight smile and a nod.

'Where's Owen?' I ask.

Jim looks surprised and I realise I've totally ignored Robert. I should speak to him but I can't seem to bring myself to; I need to know where Owen is.

'He's left the company.'

'Left? That was a bit sudden.' Why am I asking?

This is good news; Carrie's message obviously did the trick and Owen has been dealt with.

Jim doesn't answer and although my brain is saying shut up, my mouth has a mind of its own.

'Why has he left?'

Jim looks uncomfortable and won't meet my eyes and I wonder if something has happened to Owen: something bad. The thought pops into my head that the reason he's not coming back is because he's dead. I push it away, telling myself to stop being ridiculous.

'I don't know any details, Miss Enderby, just that he's not coming back.'

We stand awkwardly and the silence stretches, only broken when Robert coughs.

Without another word, I turn and walk over to the waiting lift and get in. I press the button and as the lift ascends, I wonder if there's something wrong with me. I don't feel right.

At all.

The doors open and I step outside and then stop. I turn and look around me and confusion swamps me. Something is definitely wrong; everything looks different. Small differences that I can't quite put my finger on but I know it's not the same; it doesn't feel the same. Where is the umbrella stand that is always outside the apartment nearest the lift? I see it every day; I walk past it every day. It's black with gold oriental birds painted on it. I look around, the tiny changes forcing their way into my brain. The large picture of the sunflower opposite the lift has turned into a huge, red tulip. The corridor leading to my apartment doesn't look the way it normally does and after a moment, I realise why.

It's on the wrong side; I always turn left for my door but now I have to turn right.

Terror begins to course its way through me and I close my eyes in the hope that when I open them, everything will have returned to normal. I feel myself begin to sway and I open my eyes to prevent myself from falling, putting my hand against the wall to steady myself.

What is wrong with me?

And as I stare at the wall, I begin to laugh; my hand is right next to the number four.

I'm on the wrong floor.

I quickly step back into the lift and press the number three button and wait as the doors close and we go down. As soon as the doors open, I feel better.

This is my floor.

I hurry along to my apartment and let myself in, closing and bolting the door behind me with a sigh of relief. How did I manage to press the wrong button? I've never done that before; maybe I'm more tired than I think. I pop my head through the lounge doorway but there's no sign of Carrie and I wonder how long she'll be.

I feel jittery.

I go into my bedroom and through to the en suite, suddenly purposeful, and put the plug in the bath and turn on the taps. A warm, relaxing bath is what I need to calm me down. When Carrie gets home, we could order a takeaway. A curry or a Chinese because I'm suddenly ravenous and need something substantial to eat. A smoothie or boiled eggs on toast just isn't going to cut it tonight.

I pour a generous amount of scented essential oil into the bath and quickly strip my clothes off and drop them into the laundry basket. I tie my hair up and climb into the bath. The water's too hot but I don't get out, I turn off the hot tap and turn the cold on full. When the water has nearly reached the top, I turn it off; any more and it'll overflow. I lean back, submerge myself up to my neck in the bubbles and close my eyes.

Bliss.

I open my eyes with a start. I must have dozed off; the water is stone cold and the bubbles are now a thin layer of scum on top of the water. I'm freezing; I must have been asleep for ages because my skin is wrinkled and I can barely feel the ends of my fingers. I quickly stand up, pull out the plug and climb out of the bath. After towelling myself dry, I slip on fresh underwear and pull my towelling robe on to try and stop myself from shivering.

How could I have fallen asleep for so long?

I lean over and turn on the cold tap to rinse the bath out and see something spinning around in the water as it circles the plug hole. I peer closer, trying to make out what it is.

When it comes into focus, I jump back with a cry.

It's a dead bird.

I watch the water drain away but the bird stays in the bottom of the bath on top of the plughole, its neck bent and twisted, as if it's been broken.

I can't understand how it got there.

Maybe it flew in through an open window; birds do that sometimes and then they panic when they can't get out. Except there are no windows open wide enough for a bird to get in. My bedroom window is open a fraction but it's on lock; no way could a bird get through that tiny gap.

Someone put it there whilst I was asleep.

The thought fills me with horror but it's the only explanation. It wasn't there when I got into the bath which means that someone came in here. My skin starts to crawl and I turn around, convinced that I'm being watched. There's no one there. I run out of the bathroom and pull the door shut behind me, looking wildly around the bedroom expecting someone to jump out of the wardrobe at any moment.

I can't stay in here.

I run into the lounge but there's no sign of Carrie. I wish she'd come home. I'm trying not to panic but I know that someone else is here in the apartment with me.

Someone, or something evil; I can feel it. A deafening thumping sound from the hallway startles me and my heart starts to pound; the thumping reverberates around my brain and I put my hands over my ears. Suddenly, the thumping stops and I slowly take my hands away from my ears and force myself to tiptoe over to the open lounge door and peer into the hallway.

Silence.

Boom, boom, boom! It starts again and I realise that someone or something is hammering on the front door. They're going to smash the door down to get to me. I whimper and cling onto the doorframe and then the noise stops as suddenly as it started. I hold my breath, praying that whoever or whatever is at the door will leave me alone. When the thumping suddenly starts again, I can't help myself; I open my mouth and scream as loudly as I can before sliding to the floor on knees weakened with fear. I curl my body into a ball and wrap my arms over my head as if that will save me.

The thumping stops and I brace myself for it to start again. All I can hear is the sound of my own ragged breathing.

It's quiet; maybe it's gone.

I slowly pull my arms down, raise my head and open my eyes and stare at the front door. I could make a run for it: race down the fire escape stairs. Open the door and run for my life and hope I can get by whatever or whoever is outside.

It could work.

I stand up and am about to step forward when I see the front door bulging inwards, only the bolt at the top preventing it from opening. I whimper and clap my hand over my mouth but it's no good, I can't stop the scream that escapes my mouth as whoever is on the other side of the door begins to slam against it, battering the wood against the bolt in an attempt to pull it free from its fixing. Back and forth, back and forth until the door is moving so quickly that it can only be seconds away from breaking. I hear the splinter of wood, a cracking sound as one of the screws in the bolt pulls loose. I stop screaming and begin to sob, knowing that this is it; there is no escape.

I close my eyes and screw them tightly shut.

I'm going to die.

12

'Mia? Mia? What's happened? MIA?'

I feel arms around me, pulling me to my feet. I keep my eyes tightly closed; this could be a trick.

He's trying to catch me out; make me think it's safe.

I'm pulled along, guided by the warm hands on my arms but I don't open my eyes. If I open my eyes, he'll get me.

I'm being lowered down and I feel the softness of a cushion beneath me.

'Mia. Open your eyes. Look at me.' I know that voice.

Fingers touch my face and although I don't intend to, my eyelids open involuntarily to see Carrie in front of me. Her face is red and blotchy, her hair wild.

'It's okay,' she whispers. 'I'm here now.'

I start to shiver; it starts in my feet and works its way up through my body in a wave until the shiver becomes a shake and I can't stop my teeth from chattering. Carrie gets up and seconds later returns with the throw from the arm of the chair, drapes it around my shoulders and pulls it tightly around me.

'You're in shock, Mia; take some deep breaths and the shaking will pass.'

'Where is he, Carrie?' I whisper.

'Who? Where's who?'

'Marco. He's in here somewhere, hiding. He broke the door down. He's going to kill me.'

'Marco's dead, Mia, you know that. It was me at the door; I was trying to get in. You'd put the bolt on and I couldn't get the door open but I could hear you screaming. That's why I broke in. Didn't you hear me shouting at you to let me in?'

I shake my head. 'No. It was him. He was here. I heard him.'

'No you didn't; you heard me. It was me at the door; me trying to get in, no one else.'

I turn my head and look around the lounge, my gaze stopping at the shadows in the corners where the light doesn't quite reach. The sun is going down and the room is getting darker and things suddenly make sense; Marco is dead. He is. Carrie's right. I lean closer to Carrie and whisper close to her ear so that he can't hear me.

'This flat is haunted, Carrie. Haunted. By Marco. He's come back. He's in here.'

Carrie doesn't answer and when I look at her, there are tears streaming down her face.

'Hey, don't cry.' I take her hand. 'It's okay. We're moving out, I'm buying a new house. We'll leave Marco behind and he won't be able to find us. Everyone knows that ghosts are tied to one place, so we'll be safe in a new house.'

She smiles and I feel better for a moment but then one of the shadows in the corner moves and I know he's still there, watching, waiting. He can hear me talking about him. I must be more careful.

'You need to put the light on, Carrie, and make everything bright because he doesn't like the light. Ghosts are afraid of the light.' Somehow, I know this and I feel better for knowing. Carrie gets up, walks over to the wall and flicks the switch for the ceiling light. The room is suddenly illuminated in startling white light and I blink as my eyes adjust. We never use this light; it's too white, too bright.

But not now.

'That's better. I'm feeling a lot better now; now I know what we have to do. Maybe we can get an exorcist in to get rid of him. Although there's still the bird to get rid of. Out of the bath.'

'The bird?'

'Yes. He put a dead bird in the bath while I was in there, to frighten me, but it's okay; now I know what he's trying to do, I can cope with it.'

She nods but I catch something in her eyes, something I don't like.

'You don't believe me, do you?'

'Of course I do.' She smiles. 'But first I need to look at the front door, see if it's fixable.'

I study her face to see if she's telling the truth. I'm not sure.

'Okay,' I say, feeling calmer. 'But it doesn't really matter about the door now. Not now I know.'

'Know what?'

'Marco's in here already. He's always been here; I just didn't know it.'

* * *

The smell of toast hits my nostrils as I wake and my stomach growls its response. I'm lying on the sofa and the duvet from my bed is over me. I take hold of it and throw it off because I'm sweating. It's the middle of July and not in the slightest bit cold. I sit up and hear Carrie clattering around the kitchen: the sound of the toaster, the opening and closing of the cutlery drawer, the kettle about to boil. It's as if my hearing is super-charged.

Carrie walks into the lounge with a plate of toast and stops dead in front of me and stares at me with something like fear.

'You're awake,' she says, stating the obvious. 'How do you feel? Do you want some toast? Have this and I'll do myself some more.' There's a false brightness to her tone and I recognise it; it's how people spoke to me after Gramma died. They'd ask if I was all right but I knew they didn't want to know the truth; they wanted me to tell them I was fine and that I wasn't going to burst into tears or do something embarrassing.

I never did.

'I feel strange,' I reply as she hands me the plate. 'Odd. And I have the most terrible headache. I had a horrific nightmare about Marco and don't even remember how I ended up on the sofa. Is that why I'm in here; did I wake you up?'

'Sort of,' she says, cryptically.

'And why,' I point up at the light, 'is that dreadful light on? We never have it on. It's like the O2 stadium in here.'

'You wanted me to turn it on. Don't you remember?'

'No, I don't,' I say, after thinking about it for a moment. I look down to see that I'm wearing my dressing gown. 'What time is it?'

'Half past one.'

'In the morning?'

'Yes.'

I remember putting my dressing gown on, I think. I remember falling asleep in the bath and then waking up and getting out and putting my dressing gown on. Or did I dream that? I'm not sure.

'How long have I been asleep?'

'Ages. Hours. Can you remember what happened?'

'I remember falling asleep in the bath. I think. Unless I dreamt that. I clearly remember leaving work and wanting to walk home but I don't remember why. After that, I don't know. I had a horrible nightmare about a ghost who was trying to break down the door.'

I swing my legs off the sofa and sit up properly and Carrie sits down next to me. I offer her the plate and she takes a piece of toast and I do the same and bite into it. It tastes heavenly.

'What's happened, Carrie? I know something's happened but I don't know what. I know that I definitely had another nightmare about Marco; he'd turned into a ghost and was trying to get into the house and I couldn't stop him. He was going to do something to me, kill me, I think. There was something about a dead bird too, but it's fading fast and I can't grasp all of the details.'

'Okay.' Carrie takes a bite of toast and chews it carefully. 'It wasn't a nightmare; it was real. I came home from work and I couldn't get into the flat because you'd bolted the door. I couldn't open it so I was banging on the door and shouting for you but you didn't answer.'

A vague memory of loud thumping comes back to me.

'Then what?'

'Well, then I heard you screaming. God it was awful; I thought someone had broken in and was attacking you. I was ready to call the police and had taken my phone out of my bag but the screaming seemed really close so I looked through the letterbox and there you were, standing by the lounge door screaming.'

'Oh God.' I try to remember but although there's something there, it's vague. More of a feeling than a memory.

'Then you suddenly stopped screaming and dropped to the floor and curled up into a ball. I put my phone away and battered that door for all I was worth but when I finally managed to get in, you didn't even seem to know I was here. You were convinced you were being haunted by Marco and that he was in here with us.'

'Oh my God, what the hell is happening to me, Carrie?'

'I think,' she says slowly, 'that you had some sort of episode. A mini breakdown or something. That's the only explanation I can think of.'

I put down the plate and stare into space, trying to make sense of it, trying to remember what I was thinking, but there's nothing there, just an overwhelming feeling of panic.

'On the upside,' Carrie says with a grim smile. 'Somehow, the front door lock has survived, God knows how. The bolt's broken but I'm sure Jim on security will sort it out if we slip him a few quid.'

'How bad was it?' I turn and look at her.

She hesitates before replying. 'The truth?'

I nod.

'Bad. Very bad. For a while there, I had no idea what to do. It was getting to the stage where I thought I was going to have to call someone, a doctor, or the hospital, I don't know... someone, because I had no clue what to do and I couldn't get through to you. You were absolutely convinced that Marco was in here.'

'How long did this go on for?'

'A couple of hours, maybe, although it seemed like forever. It felt like weeks. You'd stopped screaming once I was inside, but you were convinced that Marco was here, haunting the house. You started talking about exorcism, getting a priest in, stuff like that. You started scrolling through your phone looking for churches. Then you insisted I look in your bathroom at the dead bird in the bath. You said Marco had put it in the bath as a message when you were asleep. I went and looked and then came back and told you I'd disposed of it, and you didn't need to worry any more. That seemed to calm you a bit and you looked exhausted so I persuaded you to have a lie down and eventually you fell asleep.'

'Did you find the bird?'

'No.' She looks at me sadly. 'There was no bird, Mia; all that was in the bath was a pink bath scrunchie.'

Of course there was no bird; why did I even think there would be?

'I'm going mad, aren't I? Completely round the bend.'

'No, don't say that!'

'Why not?' I shrug. 'That's not the behaviour of a rational person, is it?'

I lean forward, put my head in my hands and close my eyes.

'You've accepted that your behaviour isn't normal and that's the first step.' Carrie says quietly. 'And now you need to take the next step because you can't go on like this.'

'Tell me what to do, Carrie.'

'You need to see a doctor and get help. Proper help. Because if you don't, I fear for your sanity. You know what happened last time, Mia, and you don't want to go there again.'

13

'I'm not sleeping well. I've been having awful nightmares and I think the lack of sleep is causing the anxiety.' I've said the same thing in different ways several times ever since I arrived here. If he listened properly, I wouldn't have to keep repeating myself.

I'm beginning to feel like a parrot.

Doctor Campbell looks at me intently for a moment and then reaches over and takes hold of my wrist and takes my pulse, studying his watch at the same time.

'It's a little fast.' He releases my wrist, pulls a box towards him and takes out a blood pressure monitor. I hold my arm out to him and he turns it this way and that before slipping the cuff on and sliding it up my arm. He presses a button on the monitor and the cuff begins to inflate.

'We'll take some bloods and see if anything pops up that shouldn't be there.' Doctor Campbell smiles at me before studying the reading on the monitor. 'We'll ask the nurse to do a urine sample, too, just to make sure there's nothing untoward lurking. Pop in to see nurse afterwards and she'll sort it all out for you.'

One of the good things about having private health care is that I didn't have to wait for an appointment; I rang up this morning and here I am, able to see a doctor this afternoon. The bad thing is that they're too thorough; no dishing out of a prescription the very minute you sit down. No, they're charging the earth, so they conduct every test possible. All I really want are some tablets to calm me down and help me to sleep. I think if I could just get back to normal sleeping, I'd be fine.

According to Carrie, her busy GP is printing out a prescription for her before she's even finished describing her symptoms. I didn't tell her I had a private GP and things were very different here because it would have just felt like I was rubbing my privilege in her face yet again. I'll lie and tell her that my GP had a cancellation and I just happened to ring at the right time. All the tests will be a waste of time anyway because I know that there's nothing physically wrong with me; it's all in my mind. Unless I've got a brain tumour or something; I suppose anything is possible, so it won't hurt to get thoroughly checked over.

Just as the cuff is beginning to get too tight, it deflates. He pulls it off my arm and slips it back into the box before turning to the screen and stabbing away at the keyboard.

'Your blood pressure's fine.' He turns from the screen and studies me. 'So you say you've been experiencing lapses of consciousness? Disturbed sleep? The feeling of dreaming whilst you're awake?'

'Yes.' So he *was* listening.

'And can you think of anything that might have caused this: a major life change? Too much work?'

'I split up with my boyfriend a few weeks ago,' I lie. I can't tell him it was over eight months ago because he's going to want to know why it's only now I'm having problems.

I don't know the answer to that myself.

'Hmm, I see.' He does some more finger stabbing at the keyboard and then picks up a slim torch from the desk, asks me to look upwards, leans forward and shines the beam of light into my right eye.

'No headaches, visual disturbances?' He flicks the torch to my left eye and I try not to blink.

'No.' *Apart from dead birds and dead boyfriends.*

'Periods regular? Any possibility that you could be pregnant?'

'Very regular and no, there is no possibility I could be pregnant.'

He sits back, turns to his keyboard and stabs aggressively at some more keys.

'How long have you felt like this?'

'A few weeks. I've tried all the usual things: going for long walks, a milky drink before bed. Herbal tea. No television two hours before going to bed, that sort of thing.'

'I see. Do you smoke or vape? Because nicotine is a stimulant so that could keep you awake as well as being extremely bad for you.'

'I've never smoked or vaped.'

'Good, good. And what about recreational drugs? Because they can have quite severe side effects, especially if you overdo it.'

'No, never.' Bit of a lie, because I used to enjoy the odd line or two of coke back in the day, but I don't do it now so there's no need to tell him.

'Any dark thoughts, feelings that you wish you weren't here? Voices in your head, that sort of thing?'

He smiles to take the sting out of his words, but I know why he's asking.

He's obviously read my notes.

'No,' I lie, shaking my head emphatically.

'Do you think this could be a relapse of the problems you had when your grandmother died?'

I want to laugh, I really do, but obviously I don't because I have no intention of ending up where I did after Gramma died.

'No. Definitely not. This is absolutely nothing like that.'

He sits back in his chair, the leather squeaking as he does so, steepling his fingers under his chin.

'I could prescribe you something to calm your anxiety but that would only be a temporary solution. Therapy would likely be the best option for you. You could work through your anxieties instead of trying to suppress them because it's better to get these things out in the open, rather than use drugs to deal with them. I can refer you to an excellent therapist who could fit you in almost immediately.'

'I have a very demanding job,' I lie. 'So although therapy sounds like an excellent idea, I need something now to help me sleep so I can continue to function at work.'

'I could write you a certificate. Then you could

take some time off and have a break from work for a while. Get yourself fighting fit again. It might be just what you need.'

'Impossible,' I snap. 'I have deadlines to meet and I simply cannot take time off.'

I glare at him and wonder why he's being so awkward. He knows very well that he's going to prescribe me tranquilisers because that's what I've come here for. That's the deal; I pay a fortune for private health care and he gives me what I want.

He turns to his screen again and begins to type and after a few moments, the printer at the side of the desk springs into action.

'I've prescribed you a month's supply of a mild tranquiliser. As you still have to go to work, I can't prescribe anything stronger. I really think therapy is the best option for you because tranquilisers on their own aren't the answer.'

He studies me and I try not to squirm. He's not going to let it drop so I'll have to agree to it. I won't turn up for the appointment; I'll say I forgot or make up some sort of excuse.

'Okay. If you think it will help.'

'Excellent. I'm sure it will benefit you. Reception can arrange an appointment for you and you should hear from them in the next couple of days.' He rips the paper from the printer, picks up a pen, signs it with a flourish and holds it out to me. I take it from him and stand up to leave.

'Don't forget to pop in and see the nurse for your tests.' He smiles up at me and I smile back.

'Of course.'

'Come back and see me in a month and we'll review everything and see how the therapy is helping.'

I leave his office and decide the blood tests can wait for another time. I just want to get out of here and go home but as I come out of his office, a uniformed nurse is waiting in reception. Smiling when she sees me, she comes straight over and asks me to go with her and feeling I don't have a choice, I follow her into a small room with a high bed. I do as she asks and lie down and pull up my sleeve. I bite down my irritation and hold out my arm. She inserts a needle in my arm and takes five vials of blood. I ask her what she's testing me for and she replies, 'just the usual', as if I know what she means. She then gives me a plastic cup and sends me to a door at the back of the room which turns out to be a toilet. I come back with the required sample and hand it to her and she puts it carefully on the desk behind her. She then takes me back out to reception whilst telling me that the results will be back in a couple of days.

By the time I come down the stairs and emerge into the sunshine, I feel as if I've been in there for hours. I look at my watch to see that it's actually only been forty-five minutes.

I take out my phone and order a cab from the app. I'll get him to drop me off at the cluster of shops near to my apartment because there's a chemist there. There's still plenty of time before they close so I'll be able to get the prescription filled and start taking them tonight.

I hope they work.

Maybe a therapist *would* be the answer but they'd only be able to properly help me if I could tell them the truth and that's impossible. What am I going to do if the tablets don't work?

I'll end up locked up in that place again and I'll have no say in what happens to me. Maybe I should be there, unlike last time. A therapist will be a last resort because I know how quickly events can spiral out of control; once you're in the system, it's near impossible to get out and all control over your own life vanishes.

I shudder and push the thought away. There's absolutely no point in panicking and frightening myself about it because it won't help. I have to put my faith in the tranquilisers and hope they do the trick. Right now, apart from feeling tired, I feel fine: no voices in my head, no imaginary birds, no fear that Marco is following me.

Nothing.

It's so bizarre.

Unless this is how madness is: fine one minute, deranged the next.

A cab pulls up to the pavement right next to me and I lean down next to the open window.

'Enderby?' The driver bellows.

'Yes!' I pull open the door and clamber in. One thing at a time; get the tablets and take it from there.

* * *

'I'm much better, honestly, Sebastian, don't fuss. I'll see you tomorrow.' I turn off my phone and toss it onto the bedside cabinet.

I'm in bed; not because I'm ill but because I'm getting an early night. It's only eight o'clock and Carrie's not even home yet but I'm so tired, I could sleep hanging on a washing line. I've taken a tablet and I was all ready to hunker down under the duvet and go to sleep when Sebastian rang. When I rang him this morning to tell him I wouldn't be in work because I had a migraine, I was surprised at how concerned he was. Guiltily surprised, because obviously, I was lying – although truthfully, I didn't feel exactly great after yesterday. He even suggested coming round and cooking me something to eat and looking after me. I almost slipped up and told him that I'd bought myself a sandwich from the deli next to the chemist before I remembered that I was supposed to be at home with a migraine.

I think I'll sleep. I feel quite calm after taking the tranquiliser. Although actually, I felt calm before I took it. I came into the apartment and even when I saw the splintered wood and the bolt hanging off the door frame, I didn't feel any anxiety.

It's very strange.

I put the television on for a while and watched a programme about buying a holiday home in Spain and then I got my iPad out and looked through the emails the estate agent sent me. I've found a house that I like and I think I might arrange to go and view it next weekend. Start the process of moving out of this apartment into somewhere new. Start afresh.

And all the while I was doing this, I felt absolutely fine. Normal.

I don't understand it; how can I go from deranged and climbing the walls to perfectly normal in the space of a day? It doesn't make any sort of sense. I've always assumed that if you're having some sort of breakdown, it would be all the time, not some of the time, which just shows how little I know about it.

I pull my silk eye mask over my eyes to block out the light and try to think positive thoughts.

I will sleep peacefully and wake up refreshed, I repeat to myself, over and over again.

It's just a question of mind over matter.

14

I was fine when I got to work this morning.

Absolutely fine.

But here I am, mid-afternoon, and my mood is changing; I'm jumpy and jittery and I can't seem to keep still. It's how I felt on Monday.

I need to get out of here before it gets worse because I know, with certainty, that it will.

I can hear Sebastian chatting to Debby in the main gallery room and I know that as soon as he's finished, he'll come out here to spend some time with me. We've arranged to go out for dinner tonight and I was going to stay over at his but now, that's going to be impossible. He's been in and out to chat to me since I arrived at work this morning and he even came and sat in the kitchen and spent his lunchtime with me. I think he's smitten. I'm not even sure how I feel about him because all I can think about is how I don't feel right, I don't feel normal. He's being nice but I don't want to see him now because I know I'm only going to get worse. What if I had a meltdown like I did on Monday night? How would I explain that to him?

I wouldn't be able to.

I think, in all honesty, if it happened here, a doctor would be called and events would very quickly spiral out of my control and I'd end up being sectioned.

Perhaps I need to be sectioned; perhaps I need proper help.

But I can't have proper help because how could I stop myself from confessing to murder? I couldn't. I have to get a grip on things or else I might as well walk into a police station right now and confess everything and get it over with.

I keep telling myself that I'm okay because I feel normal and then this happens and I suddenly have no control over myself. There was no nightmare last night but now Monday is repeating itself; one day of normality and it's happening all over again.

Maybe I should just confess that I killed Marco;

throw myself on the mercy of the police, tell them it was an accident, which is the truth. I didn't mean to kill him.

Except that I'd have to explain to them that Marco's body has vanished. The first question that they'd ask would be is, *If it was an accident, where's his body?* No, there's no way they'd believe it was an accident and I wouldn't blame them. I wish now that I hadn't been so useless; I should have just called the police and taken the blame for what I did, taken the blame for my stupidity.

How I rue that night. Why did it have to happen; why did Marco have to have that stupid gun? His foolish showing off, waving the gun around and bragging he was some sort of gangster who knew dangerous people. He wouldn't tell me where he'd got it from or even why he had it, except to brag that it showed he meant business. No one messed with you if you had a gun.

And I was pathetically impressed.

At first.

As so often happened with Marco, his mood suddenly flipped from boastfulness to anger. As if a switch had been flicked. It was the way he was; sometimes, I could pinpoint it to something I'd said, but mostly, I never knew why. Weirdly, this made me want him more. It was exciting, shouting and pushing each other around. It was passion, I told myself, even though it was paired with violence.

It was real.

And afterwards, there was always the making up. This was when I convinced myself underneath the nastiness, Marco loved me. I mistook lust for love but I felt alive when I was with him, fully alive. I look back now at my pitiful idolisation of him and I cringe.

Marco thought he could make me do anything he wanted – and he could. Even picking up the gun and pointing it at him was because he was taunting me. I was a privileged, gutless waste of space; a weak baby who disgusted him with my whining about being an orphan. There were people with real problems in the world, he goaded me, and I was a coward who was too afraid to even touch a gun, let alone use one. I was desperate to impress. Praise from Marco was rare and special and I hungered for it like nothing else; he was oxygen to me.

How unlucky for him that the gun was loaded.

Was the night I shot him the start of this, whatever this is? I remember feeling paranoid and jittery that night, so maybe killing Marco wasn't the start of it; maybe this was building up before that. Not that it matters now. I can't go to the police, it's too late; I'd be incriminating Carrie as well as myself. Both of our lives would be over. For some reason, this thought strikes me as hilariously funny and I clamp my hand over my mouth to stop myself from laughing out loud. My brain is zipping around in circles at a hundred miles an hour and I just want it to stop. Thoughts flash through my mind that seem important but vanish before I can catch hold of them to see what they are.

Unable to sit still, I stand up, pick up my jacket and bag and with a glance through the gallery to reassure myself that Sebastian hasn't seen me, I rush out of the building and onto the street.

I'll go straight home and take a tranquiliser; maybe it'll calm me and slow down the constant gabble in my brain. I wish now that I'd bought them with me even though I'm only supposed to take one before bedtime. I march down the street as quickly as my legs will carry me, keen to get away from the possibility of being seen by anyone in the gallery. Sebastian will wonder where I am again because I ran away last week, didn't I? Just left the gallery and ran off without a word to anyone.

But I can't bring myself to care about that.

I feel conspicuous as I hurry along, as if I stand out from the crowd and people are looking at me and whispering about me. I keep looking over my shoulder behind me, convinced that someone is hot on my heels following me.

The rapidly diminishing rational part of me knows that I'm not being followed; it's in my head.

It's not real.

Even knowing this, that it's paranoia and isn't real, my body refuses to listen. My heart is racing as if it will burst out of my chest and the thought explodes in my brain that I'm going to die. Panic almost overwhelms me. I swallow and my mouth is so dry, it's painful. I increase my speed to a near-run, the only thought in my mind to get home and take a tablet.

What if it doesn't work?

It has to work. It's my only chance. I look down and concentrate on my feet; one foot in front of the other, over and over again. Focus Mia, focus and just get yourself home.

By the time I reach the apartment building, I've start to knock into people as I walk, stumbling around like a drunk. The first few times, I mumbled an apology but after a while, it became too much effort and I wanted to laugh at the annoyed faces that loomed over me.

Somehow, I manage to punch in the code on the entry system, or maybe whoever's at the desk presses the door release button. I don't know, don't care, but at least I'm in. I run through reception, barely registering the new security man at the desk. I should know his name; someone told me, I think.

I can't remember.

I get into the lift and stare at the buttons and put my finger on number three and press it. Nothing happens. I stab at it but my finger seems to be made of rubber, so I resort to covering the button with my palm and leaning on it. After forever, the doors close and the lift moves upwards.

Time jumps around in a weird way and suddenly, I'm in the flat; standing in the hallway although I don't remember how I got here. The front door is closed and locked but I can't bolt it; the bolt is broken. I'm staring at the bolt as if looking at it will repair it, and walk angrily down the hallway to my bedroom when it refuses to comply. I go straight over to the bedside cabinet and pull open the drawer. I need to take a tablet now. I need this to stop.

The tablets aren't there.

I rummage around the drawer with increasing dread. They're gone. Someone has taken them.

Marco.

I push him away and try to think where the tablets might be; I must have put them somewhere else.

Think.

I look wildly around the room, narrowing my eyes as if it will help me to see them. A sudden thought hits me: the bathroom, I took them with a glass of water last night. I dash into the bathroom and there they are, lying on the side of the sink. I dash across, pick them up and with trembling fingers pop a tablet out and push it into my mouth. I swallow it down and it feels as if I'm swallowing a golf ball. The half-empty glass of water is still on the shelf where I left it last night and I pick it up and gulp down the lukewarm liquid.

Now I have to wait for it to work.

If it works.

I go back into the bedroom but, when I see the bed, the thought of lying on it fills me with terror, so I go out into the hallway and cross into the lounge. If I turn on the television, that might help; it'll take away the terrifying silence and the sound of my own breathing. I pick up the remote control, point it at the television and press it in the same moment that the wall in front of me ripples like water. Then the room begins to spin, slowly at first and then faster and faster until the walls and furniture are a blur of colour. I stumble around and try to steady myself but it's no good. As the room darkens and I begin to fall to the floor, the last coherent thought in my mind is that maybe I shouldn't have taken the tranquiliser.

* * *

I open my eyes and stare up at the ceiling.

Satisfied that the room has stopped spinning, I slowly pull myself upright and look around. The light is fading and I hold my wrist up in front of my face and stare at my watch. When I eventually manage to focus on it, I see that it's twenty past seven. I must have been asleep, or unconscious, for hours. As I lower my hand, I wince; my elbow is sore and I guess I hit it on something when I fell. My mouth is dry, I'm desperate for a drink and my forehead throbs with the promise of a monumental headache.

I pull myself to my feet and sit down gingerly on the sofa but almost immediately get up again and run for the bathroom. I just manage to pull the toilet seat up before I vomit profusely. Just when I think

I've finished, I vomit again and I hang over the toilet bowl and watch as everything I've eaten and drunk over the past few days flows from me. Looking at the disgusting mess makes me vomit again until eventually, all I can do is dry heave. There can be nothing left inside of me. I flush the toilet and pull myself up from the floor feeling unbelievably weak and shaky. The promise of the headache has now become a reality. I lean back against the wall and close my eyes in the hope that the pounding in my head will subside.

I need fluids, I decide, because I must be dehydrated and as I have that thought, I realise something else.

I feel normal again.

Physically, I feel like shit, but mentally, the paranoid feelings that propelled me home have gone. Completely. I'm no longer afraid of something or looking in dark corners imagining that someone is there waiting to get me. I don't feel jittery or confused.

I scramble up from the floor, go over to the basin and rinse my mouth out with water and then splash some over my face. When I pick up the towel to dry myself, I catch sight of my reflection in the mirror.

I look like a ghost: an ashen, wild-eyed, dishevelled ghost.

I dry my face and go into the hallway and through to the kitchen. I turn on the tap and fill a glass with water and drink it straight down. I fill the glass again but don't drink it; I need to make sure it's not going to come straight back up again before I drink any more. I sit down on one of the bar stools at the breakfast bar that Carrie and I rarely use, and slowly sip the water. Should I eat something? I've hardly eaten today, just a slice of toast and a smoothie and that's all come up now; there's nothing left in my stomach. I should line my stomach with something, but not yet, later; I don't want a repeat of the vomiting.

A blast of music makes me jump and I realise it's the television from the lounge. I drink the rest of the water, making myself sip it slowly. A jingle plays from an advert as I get up and then head out into the hall-way. I'm halfway to the lounge when the doorbell rings. I breathe a sigh of relief; it'll be Carrie. I walk unsteadily to the front door and unlock and open it at the very second that it occurs to me that Carrie wouldn't ring the bell because she has a key.

'Hello, Mia.'

I stare up into the face of Owen, his expression full of anger and rage and something else that I can't put my finger on. I immediately try and push the door closed but I'm no match for a man his size. He shoves the door inwards and I stumble backwards, just managing to stay on my feet. He steps into the hallway and hurls the door closed behind him and glares at me.

'Well, this is cosy, isn't it?'

15

My feet are rooted to the spot and I feel terror surge through me as Owen walks towards me. He's even taller than I remember and I feel dwarfed in his presence; he can easily overpower me. Breaking free of my inertia, I dash through the open doorway into the lounge and shove the door closed behind me to give myself a few seconds more. I look wildly around, but for what, I'm not sure.

Something, anything. A weapon? A way out?

There is nothing in here that I can use to defend myself with unless I batter him with a sofa cushion and the only way in, or out, of this apartment is the front door. The sofa: I could climb behind it, use it as a barrier, put it between me and him.

But I'd also be trapped and unable to move.

I spot my handbag lying on the floor in front of the sofa where I left it and I scrabble towards it. My phone must be inside because I haven't used it since I got home. If I'm quick, I can ring the police and leave the line open so they can hear what's going on; I can shout the address out or something. I unzip the bag with trembling fingers and thrust my hand inside and fumble around for the familiar contours of my phone. My fingers touch the outline of the screen almost immediately and I think that, yes, there is a god. I grab hold of the phone and am pulling it out when I hear the lounge door fly open and rebound off the wall with a bang. I have only seconds before Owen reaches me. But it's already too late; the bag is roughly ripped from my hands and I look up to see him towering over me. He thrusts the handbag underneath his armpit and clamps his arm down over it, making it impossible for me to get to it. If I wasn't so terrified, it would be funny because he looks ridiculous: a huge man mountain holding a woman's handbag underneath his arm.

I take several steps backwards in an attempt to put some space between us.

'You can't just force your way in here,' I say. 'It's against the law.'

'Is that right?' He grins. 'Because it seems like I just did exactly that.'

He takes another step towards me and I step back again and feel the ridge of the coffee table pressing into the back of my legs. I'm trapped and unable to move away from him.

'What do you want, Owen?' I ask. My voice is wobbly and tears aren't far away. 'Why are you here?'

'Don't pretend you don't know.'

'I don't, Owen. Honestly. I don't.'

He laughs bitterly.

'Really? You actually think you can lie your way out of this? There's no point in even trying because I know what you did. Don't go thinking you can flutter your eyelashes at me and play the innocent and I'll believe your lies. I know the truth.'

He shouldn't be here; Carrie was going to get a message to the guy about Owen. Let them know that someone else knew about Marco. Do something about him. And it must have worked in some way because Owen doesn't work here any more, does he? Jim told me so. They dealt with it and he was gone. So why is he here? He must know what sort of people he's dealing with: how dangerous they are, how much danger he's now in for going against them. As

Carrie says, no one argues with them because the consequences are harsh.

But that's not going to help me now, is it? And maybe Owen isn't afraid of them; maybe he's even more dangerous than they are. Maybe, he's one of them.

'Haven't you got anything to say?' he demands.

'How did you get into the building?' I ask, stalling for time.

He laughs. 'Well, it wasn't difficult, was it? Seeing as I know the code. I used to work here, remember? Before I got the sack.' He studies me for a moment. 'Don't waste your time thinking that the new bloke on security is going to save you because he didn't even see me. He's a lazy arse. He spends most of his time skiving in the toilet so he has no idea I'm here. No one knows I'm here, Mia; it's just you and me.'

'I'm sorry, Owen. I'm sorry. Really sorry. About what happened.'

'And that's it? You're sorry?' He shakes his head in disbelief. 'You say you're sorry and that makes it okay, does it? You're one spoilt, entitled bitch and you have no fucking idea what you've done. You've ruined my life.'

His mouth twists into an ugly line and the man in front of me bears no resemblance to the smiling, affable Owen who used to try and engage me in conversation every time I walked through the foyer.

'All I can say is that I'm sorry. I wish it hadn't happened and I wish with all my heart that I could go back and change it, but I can't.'

He frowns slightly and I wonder long it will be until Carrie comes home. *Please Carrie*, I silently beg, *come home now and save me. Please.*

'What do you want?' I ask, as he continues to stare at me, a slightly puzzled look on his face. And then it hits me: money. Of course he wants money because why else would he be here?

Blackmail.

It's so blindingly obvious that I can't believe I didn't think of it sooner.

'What do you think I want, Mia?'

'I can pay,' I say. 'I can get you money. A lot of money. Just tell me how much.'

'Money?' His voice is quieter now. 'Let me see. Ten grand. No, twenty grand? How about that?'

It's a lot, and he could come back for more. He will come back for more but even knowing that, I'm going to tell him I'll pay it because then he'll go. I don't feel so afraid now; once I've convinced him that I'll send him the money, he'll leave. Carrie will have to get in touch with them, again, and they'll have to do something about him to stop him from coming back.

'Twenty,' I say. 'I'll give you twenty. Give me your bank details and I'll arrange it. You'll have it in your account tomorrow.'

He bursts out laughing: loud, raucous laughter. I wait for him to finish.

'You think you can pay me off?' He steps closer; his anger is almost palpable. I smell alcohol, too. He's been drinking. 'You actually think that's what I came here for?'

He tosses my handbag behind him and takes hold of the tops of my arms, his fingers biting into the flesh, and I stare up at him in confusion. What does he want? I don't understand what he could possibly want if it's not money. My brain is firing in all directions, trying to think of a way out of this, a way to get him to leave, but nothing makes sense, nothing.

'I don't know. I don't know why you came here. Please tell me what it is you want and I'll give it to you.'

My insides turn to water as it sinks in that, if it isn't money, it's something else. Maybe he wants to hurt me, humiliate me. Rape me because I spurned his advances, because I didn't fall at his feet. He could be one of those men who can't take rejection; can't believe that a woman can turn them down. He could rape me and I wouldn't be able to stop him or tell anyone, because he knows what I did, he knows my secret. I swallow down the bile that rises in my throat and pray yet again for Carrie to come home.

He pushes his face to within inches of mine and I feel his breath on my face.

'I'll tell you what I want, Mia. I want revenge. Revenge. Do you understand now?'

16

'Revenge?' I ask, staring into his eyes. My brain tries to process what he's saying. Blackmail I could understand, rape, even, if he thinks that he should take what I won't give. But revenge? For what? Revenge isn't the dark web; revenge is personal.

He knew Marco. The thought hits me like a missile out of nowhere. Because that would make it personal. They were friends. I killed his friend.

No, more than that. It must be more than that; knowing Marco isn't enough.

What was it he said? I'd ruined his life. Why would he say that? How would killing Marco ruin Owen's life?

Comprehension slowly dawns as I stare up into

his face: the dark eyes, the coil of springy, black hair that falls over his forehead. The hair that reminded me so much of Marco. Of course. There's a reason that he reminded me of Marco, that they look so alike.

Owen is related to Marco.

They're family.

Cousins or brothers. No amount of money is going to save me now; there is nothing I can do. I've murdered someone he loved, and Owen has found out and now he's come for revenge. I've blown a family apart with my stupidity and I have to pay.

'I'm sorry,' I gasp. 'Do whatever you have to do. I deserve it.'

I close my eyes and pray that it's quick; I'm a coward and I don't want to suffer. There's nothing I can say or do to stop this now. I feel the pressure of his fingers on my arms loosen as he lets go and for a moment, I relish the freedom, but then his hands are around my throat, and I squeeze my eyes more tightly shut, praying for it to be over.

Just do it.

The pressure around my neck is suddenly relaxed and I stagger to stop myself from overbalancing and falling over.

My eyes fly open.

Owen's gone. He's not there. I lurch unsteadily and spin around, expecting him to be behind me. He's not. Taking shuddering breaths, I look wildly around the room and am shocked to see him sitting in the middle of the sofa, his head in his hands.

I could run; I should run.

But I don't. I'm too afraid and my legs won't work. In two giant strides, he could stop me. Maybe I can reason with him, tell him how sorry I am, because he stopped, didn't he? He could have killed me, if he wanted to.

'I'm sorry about Marco, Owen,' I gasp. 'So sorry.'

He looks up at me, rubbing his hand over his face. 'What?'

'I'm so sorry about Marco...'

'Who's Marco?' He cuts across me. 'What are you talking about?'

I stare at him in confusion.

'Who's Marco?' he repeats.

The anger on his face has been replaced by puzzlement. Something clicks in my brain and I realise that I've got this wrong. I've got it all wrong.

'What do you want, Owen?' I ask, my voice hoarse. 'Why did you come? Why do you want revenge?'

He shakes his head. 'You know why. I wanted to

frighten you. I just wanted to frighten you.' He doesn't look threatening or angry now, just exhausted. Spent.

'But why?'

He shakes his head. 'I've made it worse now, haven't I? You'll call the police and I'll get arrested and I'll never get another job. Ever. I'll go to prison.'

'What do you think I've done, Owen? Please tell me because I really don't know.' I lower myself onto the armchair opposite him. A safe distance away.

'You got me fired.'

'I didn't.'

He gives a snort of disbelief.

'Okay,' I say slowly. 'I need you to tell me exactly what you think I've done. I don't want to call the police and report this because I thought we were friends and I'm sure it's some sort of misunderstanding. But I need to be sure that it will never happen again.' It's a bit of a stretch saying we're friends, but I need to know what's going on. Also, I won't be calling the police. The further I keep away from them, the better. The way I've been behaving lately, I might blurt out a confession without intending to. I can't trust myself.

He looks up, a hopeful look in his eyes.

'You rang head office and made a complaint

about me. The first time, I got a warning. That's why I wouldn't help you when you wanted to look at the CCTV. When you rang them again, they fired me. Instant dismissal for inappropriate behaviour. You said I was creepy and made you feel uncomfortable.'

'Owen, you have to believe me, I never made a complaint about you. I never would.'

He looks down at the floor.

'I'll be ringing them and having a word with them,' I say. 'Because for some reason, they're lying to you and they shouldn't be going around blaming me for something I haven't done.'

'They didn't tell me; they wouldn't. Data protection or some crap. But Jim knew. He told me, on the quiet. He said I deserved to know because it wasn't fair. Why would they tell Jim it was you if it wasn't?' His tone says he thinks I'm lying.

'I don't know. But I'm going to find out because I don't like being blamed for something I didn't do.'

Incredibly, I feel calm now. Gone are the fear and certainty of only a few minutes ago that Owen would kill me. He thinks I got him sacked. While my thoughts were firing off at ridiculous tangents about Marco, it was nothing to do with him.

'Do you believe me when I say it wasn't me?'

'Don't know.' He shrugs and looks at the floor.

'You had your hands around my throat. I thought I was going to die.'

'I'm sorry. I wasn't thinking straight and I'd had a few drinks.' He sounds pathetic and a surge of anger courses through me.

'Get out.' I stand up. 'GET OUT!'

He doesn't move and I experience a second of fear; maybe I've misjudged this, maybe he's still a threat. He switched from aggressive to calm in a millisecond; what's to stop him switching back? I stand still, hardly daring to breathe as he stands up from the sofa. He towers over me, and I'm reminded how much bigger and more powerful he is than me. I take a sideways glance at the doorway, estimating if I can make it to the front door before he catches me.

'I'm sorry,' he says, quietly. 'Really sorry.'

'You need to leave.'

He nods. 'I'm going.' He turns towards the door and then stops. 'Are you going to report me to the police?'

'No.'

'Thank you. I'm so sorry. I would never have hurt you.'

'Just go.'

He walks towards the doorway and out into the hallway. I follow behind him, on legs that feel like jelly. Just a few more steps and he'll be gone. He reaches the front door, puts his hand on the lock and turns to me. I stare back at him, forcing myself not to crumble. He pulls his face into what looks like an apologetic smile.

'It's okay, Owen. I won't report you, I promise.' It feels as if someone else is speaking. Is this what an out of body experience feels like?

He turns, opens the door and steps outside, pulling the door closed behind him. I run to the door, push it to make sure it's shut and collapse in a heap in front of it, my legs unable to hold me up for a second longer. I start to cry, great heaving sobs of relief as the pent-up terror leaves my body.

It's okay.

It's all going to be okay.

17

I wake with a start. There's a moment of disorientation before I realise that my mobile phone is ringing from the bedside table. I reach out my arm and drag it towards me. Sunlight is streaming through the curtains and the room already feels hot. I wonder what the time is. I hold the phone in front of my eyes and, through blurry vision, press the button to accept the call.

'Miss Mia Enderby?' I don't recognise the voice.

'Speaking.'

'Good morning, Miss Enderby, this is Grace from Doctor Campbell's surgery.' She pauses and I guess I'm supposed to say something, so I oblige.

'Hello.' I stifle a huge yawn, hoping she hasn't heard me.

'We've received the results of your blood tests and Doctor Campbell would like you to come in to discuss them with him.'

I think about it for a moment.

'No need,' I say. 'Just tell me the results over the phone. That'll be fine.'

There's a pause before she speaks. 'I'm sorry, Miss Enderby, I'm not able to do that. Doctor Campbell is the only person who can discuss the results with you.'

I push down my irritation; I can do without pointless visits to my doctor just so he can charge me for another visit.

'Get him to call me.'

'He really would like to see you, Miss Enderby.'

I sigh. 'Okay. Schedule an appointment and let me know.' I might turn up. If I remember.

'Doctor Campbell can fit you in this afternoon at two o'clock if that's suitable?'

'That's no good, I'm busy today,' I lie. 'Next week would be better for me.'

'Um...' She dithers for a moment. 'Doctor Campbell did stress to me that it would be best if you came in today.'

'Sorry, today is out of the question.'

'If it's really impossible for you today, how about tomorrow morning at ten o'clock?'

'Why the rush? It's nothing urgent, is it?'

My reply is met with silence and I realise.

It is urgent.

'Okay, Grace. I'll come in tomorrow.'

I end the call and sit myself up in bed.

Urgent: what does that mean?

Maybe I should have gone in today to find out. Perhaps there's something seriously wrong with me that will explain the weird episodes I've been having. It would be a good thing if there was a reason, as long as it was curable. But realistically, I don't believe that I need to see him urgently at all; Doctor Campbell has called me in urgently in the past to inform me that I'm anaemic and need to start taking iron tablets, so I'm not unduly alarmed. I glance down at my phone screen to see there are loads of messages and as I'm about to open them, I notice the time: ten thirty.

I've slept for nearly fourteen hours.

After picking myself up from the floor by the front door last night, I stumbled into the bedroom and crawled into bed, so exhausted that even the thought of Owen coming back again failed to keep me awake. I had no intention of going into work today but nevertheless, I'm shocked that I've slept for so long. I never heard Carrie come home last night and she'll have left for work hours ago. Sebastian will be wondering where I am. Several of the messages are from Sebastian and I open them up; he's asking how I am and sounds concerned which isn't surprising as I haven't told him I won't be coming into work today. I'll have to lie and pretend I have a recurrence of the migraine, although despite having a raging thirst and feeling slightly sick, I feel better than I've felt in weeks. I had a lot of dreams last night but no nightmares. I can't remember much about the dreams now, but Owen featured in them. He was circling around in my head along with everything else and even now, what I've discovered seems bizarre, to say the least. I feel much calmer about what happened now. I don't think Owen did intend to hurt me; I think, as he said, he wanted to frighten me.

He certainly did that.

What I can't understand is why Jim told him it was me who reported him; why would he do that? It must be some sort of mix up at head office and I'll be having words with Jim when he comes back on shift because aside from it being a lie, he shouldn't be giving out information like that, particularly to the person involved. Especially when it's the wrong information. Although he couldn't have expected that Owen was going to storm his way into my apartment and confront me.

I've no idea who made the complaint, but really, it could be anyone. There are a lot of apartments in this building and maybe he was over-familiar with one of the other residents and they didn't like it. It seems like a harsh overreaction to report him but not everyone's like me; some women take offence at over-friendliness and feel uncomfortable with it. I think Owen's visit was fuelled by alcohol because I definitely smelled it on him, but that doesn't excuse his bursting in here and threatening me. I was genuinely terrified. It's going to be difficult for him to get another job without a reference so I can see why he thought I'd ruined his life.

But the other question that I'm forced to ask myself is, did I make a complaint to the management company and then forget I'd done so? It's perfectly possible because I've seen and heard things that are a figment of my imagination, haven't I? I need to check, but if I did do it, can I retract it – or would that look entirely mad? Owen shouldn't have to lose his job because of my strange episodes. My finger is hovering over the recent calls list on my phone to check, when it starts to ring. Sebastian's name flashes up. My first instinct is to ignore it but if I don't answer, he'll keep ringing.

I don't want to speak to him or anyone, but I'll have to. I press the button to answer.

'Hi Sebastian.'

'Mia, how are you feeling? I've been so worried about you.'

'I'm not feeling great, to be honest. It's this awful migraine, I can't seem to shift it. All I can do is rest and wait for it to go; that's what I usually do,' I lie.

'Poor you. I never knew you suffered with migraines.' There's a hint of accusation in his tone and I wonder if he knows I'm lying.

'I rarely get them but when I do, they're pretty awful. I'll be fine in a few days. I'm so sorry that I dashed off like that yesterday without saying anything.'

'It doesn't matter; I'm just worried about you. I could come over at lunchtime, make you something to eat, keep you company, cheer you up?'

He's trying to be nice, I know that, but I don't want to see him. I don't want to have to make normal conversation. I've so much going around in my head from yesterday that I'll have difficulty concentrating on small talk.

'That's really sweet of you but I'll be asleep. That's the only way I can get over it.'

'Oh. What about this evening after I finish work?'

When did he get so needy? I feel irritation rise that he won't take the hint that I don't feel up to seeing him. Marco was never needy. I was the needy one. I couldn't get enough of him; the more disinterested he was, the more obsessed with him I became.

What does that say about me?

Nothing good.

'Sorry, Sebastian, but I'm intending knocking myself out with some more painkillers and having an early night. Once I've got rid of this, we can get back to normal.' *Now please leave me alone.*

I can hear his disappointment as we say our goodbyes and I decide that the next time he rings, I won't answer. I'll let him assume I'm asleep. I sit for a moment to try to remember what I was doing when he rang and then remember I was checking my outgoing calls. I scroll through my phone and flick open the recent call records and scroll back over the last couple of weeks, just to be sure, studying each call carefully to be sure I don't miss it. There is no record of any call made to the management company's head office. I flick open the email app and repeat the process, checking all sent emails and the result is the same: nothing.

Jim's got some explaining to do.

* * *

I've dressed and showered and forced a slice of toast down, even though it tasted as if I was eating cardboard. Despite my stomach growling with hunger, when I'd gone to the bother of toasting two slices of bread and buttering them, it was as much as I could do to eat just one of them. I took one of my pre-made smoothies out of the fridge but put it back again without even taking the lid off; I've completely lost my appetite.

I'm in the foyer, waiting to speak to Jim. He's just taken a delivery in from a courier and is stowing it away in his office. I wait by the desk, mentally rehearsing what I'm going to say to him and trying to get it straight in my head. He shouldn't have repeated something that head office told him in confidence and he should definitely have got his facts right before he told Owen.

He emerges from the office and gives me his usual tight-lipped smile. Or is it more tight-lipped than usual because he thinks I got Owen dismissed? It's difficult to tell; Jim's expression never gives much away.

'Morning, Miss Enderby. Something I can help you with?'

'Well, I hope so Jim. It's about Owen.'

His expression doesn't change but there's a flicker of his eyes that he doesn't quite manage to hide.

'Owen?'

'Yes. Owen who used to work here.'

There's an uncomfortable silence and I hold Jim's gaze.

'I wondered,' I say, slowly, 'why you told him that I'd made a complaint about him to head office.' He looks puzzled and I can see that he's wondering how I know. 'Owen confronted me with what he thought I'd done, and he wasn't very happy about it,' I say, suddenly angry. 'And neither am I. I don't care for being accused of something that has nothing to do with me.'

'Owen spoke to you?' Jim looks worried.

'Yes, he did, and it wasn't a pleasant conversation. You shouldn't have told him what head office told you, Jim, especially as it wasn't true. I'm sure they wouldn't be very pleased if I contacted them and told them what you'd done. I don't think that would go very well for you, would it?'

'I'm really sorry,' Jim says, his face flushing red. 'I never meant for him to say anything to you about it. Head office wouldn't tell him who had made the complaint; just that he'd as he'd already had a warning and ignored it, he was being dismissed. They told me though, and no, I shouldn't have told him but it just sort of slipped out when he was talking to me about it. He was a nice lad and was really cut up about it. I felt a bit gutted for him, truth be told, because I don't think he deserved to lose his job.'

'I see. Okay. Well, you obviously got it wrong and misunderstood what they told you, because it definitely wasn't me.'

Jim doesn't say anything; I thought at the very least he'd apologise. I could make a complaint about him but do I really want to be that vindictive? One person has already lost their job; why make it worse?

'That's it, then,' I say, when it becomes apparent that no apology is going forthcoming. 'There's no more to be said, really, is there?'

Jim looks relieved and I turn to leave.

'I never told Owen it was you, though,' Jim says.

'What?' I turn back to face him.

'Head office never gave me a name. They just said the complaint came from apartment twenty-five.'

18

Should be home by six, I'm sick of work! x

I reread Carrie's last message to me that she sent at three o'clock this afternoon when I asked her if she was going to be late tonight.

It's now a quarter to seven.

I've been wandering around the apartment for the last few hours after my visit to Jim and I feel jittery and all over the place. My brain is a jumble of thoughts and I just want everything to be straight in my head. I feel confused and unable to think straight, which isn't surprising after the last few days. I'm about to message Carrie again when I hear the sound of her key in the front door. I stand up from the sofa, about to rush out into the hallway, and then sit down again.

For God's sake, let her get in and settled before demanding to know whether she was the one who put the complaint in about Owen. It's hardly urgent, is it? Is it even important? No, probably not. When Jim said apartment twenty-five, I assumed that he'd made a mistake, because that's the number of my apartment and I definitely didn't make a complaint, not even when I was having one of my episodes, because I checked. Jim was adamant that he wasn't mistaken and asked me to wait for a moment while he went into his office to check his email. I waited patiently by the security desk, confident that he'd return red-faced and embarrassed and admit that he'd made a blunder.

He didn't.

He came back and said that the email definitely said apartment twenty-five and if I wanted, he'd print it off and show me. I nearly said yes, print it, before realising how ridiculous that would make me sound. I left him and came back upstairs and it dawned on me that it must have been Carrie because she lives here, too. She must have been the one who contacted them. I wanted to message her and ask her immediately but managed to stop myself; she knows nothing of Owen's visit yesterday and I need to tell her about that first.

'Hey.' She walks into the lounge. 'One more day and it's the weekend. Are you okay? Did you manage to sleep your headache off?'

I'm confused for a moment before remembering that I messaged her the same lie as Sebastian this morning to account for still being in bed when she left for work.

'Much better.' I smile. 'Good day?'

'Better now today's over. Bloody people and their money.' She collapses onto the sofa next to me and stretches her legs out and wiggles her toes. 'Not too much more to do, so I'm definitely having some time off, important meetings next week or not. They can get stuffed. Randoll Finance have had more than their money's worth out of me this week. Every week, actually.'

'You're actually going to take time off?' I ask in disbelief; Carrie never has weekends off.

'Well, Sunday definitely. I'll have to go in on Saturday to finish everything off but I'm having Sunday off even if I have to work until midnight on Saturday.' She puts her head back on the sofa and closes her eyes. 'But let's not talk about work; it's depressing. Do you fancy a takeaway tonight or are you seeing Sebastian? I didn't even have time for lunch today and I'm absolutely starving.'

'No, I'm not seeing him tonight; I'll catch up with him tomorrow night. Takeaway sounds good.' The thought of food makes me shudder; I cannot face eating anything.

'I fancy pizza,' Carrie says. 'Dough balls and everything. A proper carb-fest followed by something with gooey chocolate smothered all over it.'

'Owen turned up at the door yesterday,' I blurt out.

Carrie opens her eyes and swings around to face me, a surprised look on her face. No, more than surprised: alarmed.

'He came here? What for?' she demands.

'He wanted to know why I'd reported him to head office for inappropriate behaviour. He's been fired.'

Carrie stares at me for a moment, her face a picture of concern, her cheeks flushed. 'What did you say?'

'I said I didn't know what he was talking about, which I didn't, because I did no such thing. It was you, wasn't it, Carrie?'

'What was me?'

'You reported him, but he thought it was me.'

She nods. 'Well, yes, of course it was me. What else did he say?'

'He blamed me for getting him fired and said he wanted revenge. That was pretty much the gist of it, over and over again. He'd had a few drinks to give him the courage to come here.'

'How did he know? The management company told him? That's disgusting! I'm going to make a complaint; they shouldn't be giving information out like that. Are you okay? Was he really horrible to you?' She looks at me with concern.

'I'm fine. He was fine,' I lie. 'Head office never told him; Jim did, because he felt sorry for him and thought he deserved to know. He had no idea that Owen was going to come up here and confront me. But why did you report him, Carrie? I thought you were going to contact your guy and get him to sort it out.' I sound whiney when I say it and also slightly accusing.

Carrie sighs. 'You came to me in a panic because he'd told you he knew about Marco so I sorted it. I thought that contacting the company's head office would be better for Owen than letting them deal with him. Owen would have lost more than his job if I'd left it to them, Mia. They act fast and make sure that people don't get the opportunity to cross them twice. I was doing Owen a favour: a massive favour. I didn't tell you the details because you had enough on your plate. But Owen was gone, which was what we wanted.'

'He didn't even know about Marco.'

'What?'

'He didn't know. He had no idea what I was talking about when I said I was sorry about Marco.' I don't tell her I thought he was his brother or cousin; I feel ridiculous now and almost wish I hadn't told her that he even came here because what was the point? She did what she had to do because we thought he'd found out about Marco. Unfortunately for me, Jim decided to poke his nose in and Owen put two and two together and made five. I feel exhausted talking about it and trying to explain and actually, it doesn't even matter now.

'So what exactly did you say to him?' Carrie looks thoughtful.

'I told him I was sorry about what had happened about Marco and he blatantly didn't have a clue what I was talking about.'

'Well, that's a good thing,' she says. 'That he doesn't know anything. And he's gone now, so no harm done.'

Well, he's lost his job so there's harm done to

Owen. Maybe I should tell her how frightened I was, but the effort all seems too much; it's over now so what's to be achieved by going over it all again? Besides, it'll just make her feel bad that I got the blame for something she did, and Carrie was doing it for me, wasn't she? And I'm feeling a lot better now. My thinking process is sluggish and slow but aside from that, the nightmares have stopped. I'm no longer acting like a mad person. A few days and I'll be totally back to normal. I can properly put all this behind me.

Time to put it to bed and move on.

'You're right,' I say, scrolling through my phone. 'So what's it going to be: Hawaiian, meat feast, or both?'

* * *

'Can I get you a coffee or anything, Miss Enderby?' Grace is hovering in front of me and I bite down my impatience and wave her away with an 'I'm fine,' and a smile. She's been flapping around me ever since the hour hand of the clock on the wall passed ten o'clock by a millimetre. *It's only ten past, for God's sake; get a grip, don't fuss so much.*

'I'm fine, Grace, I'll just sit here.'

'I'm really sorry about this. Doctor Campbell never normally lets his appointments overrun like this. He shouldn't be much longer.'

'It's fine,' I repeat.

'While you're here,' she says. 'Would you like to book your appointment with the therapist? She has an opening first thing on Monday morning.'

'Sorry,' I say, crisply. 'I'm in meetings all day on Monday. Could you email me some dates and I'll take a look at them?'

She hesitates for a moment. 'Um, okay.'

'Thank you.' I smile, again, and then look down at my phone so she'll take the hint that the conversation is over and leave me alone. After a moment, I hear her scuttle back to her desk and then the faint tapping of keys as she resumes typing. I stare at my phone but I'm not really looking at anything. I didn't sleep very well last night, despite taking a tranquiliser – thankfully, no nightmares – but the events of the last couple of days were playing on my mind. The whole Owen thing has left me feeling unsettled and slightly depressed. I should be feeling more stable now that it's been sorted and Carrie's explained it, but for some reason, I don't. I feel bad that Owen's lost his job but I'm not going to beat myself up over it because doing that won't change anything; it won't get him his job back. However, there's something niggling away at the back of my mind that feels as if it's important, but I can't seem to put my finger on what it is; I have a fear that this feeling is the start of another episode. It's different from the paranoia that seems to preclude the hallucinations and feelings of panic, but there's definitely something there and it's unnerving. I've been feeling fine and normal, mental-health-wise, but I've been fine before and then had a complete meltdown. Am I on the road to recovery? I desperately hope so. I do wonder whether the tranquilisers are giving me brain fog and dulling my thinking process, because it feels as if my brain is full of cotton wool. I must remember to ask Doctor Campbell when I eventually get in there, before he dishes out a prescription for iron tablets or whatever it is that he's called me in here for.

The noise of his door opening makes me look up and there he is, holding the door whilst a tiny old lady, hunched over nearly double, shuffles her way through the doorway and along to the reception desk. He walks behind her and overtakes her in two strides to lean over the desk and mutter something to Grace, who listens for a moment and then leaps up from her seat as if she's been scalded and proceeds to shout at the old lady, who I presume is deaf.

'Miss Enderby?' Doctor Campbell turns and smiles in my direction and I slip my phone into my pocket and get up.

'Sorry for the delay,' he says, as I follow him into his office and he closes the door behind me. 'The last appointment ran on a little.'

He manoeuvres himself behind his desk and resumes his seat and I sit down opposite him.

'And how are you today?'

'Okay,' I say.

'And how are the confusion and nightmares?'

'I'm coping. I'm not expecting any major improvement just yet, but I have been sleeping better. Do the tranquilisers you've prescribed me have any side effects, though? I've been finding it a little difficult to concentrate.'

'In what way?'

'At work. Sort of a brain fog; I don't feel as sharp as usual. A bit forgetful.'

'They can make you feel that way to start with but once your body adjusts to them, you should be fine. It's early days and these things can take time to settle down. You could try taking them earlier in the evening if the brain fog doesn't improve. And although the medication will help, it's not the entire answer; therapy will be most beneficial. I believe you have an appointment on Monday morning?'

'No, I haven't. As I've already informed Grace, I have important meetings all day and can't simply drop them to attend a therapy session.' The cheek of the man thinking he can organise my time for me. I have no intention of having any sort of therapy and will simply ignore Grace's emails until she gives up and stops sending them.

Doctor Campbell makes a disapproving harumph noise and I ignore him.

'I believe you have my blood test results?' I ask.

He frowns and shuffles a few papers on his desk. 'Yes, the blood and urine results came back yesterday and there appear to be a few, ahem, points for discussion.'

'You've found something wrong with me?'

'No, not as such. More of an incompatibility that I need to make you aware of. I couldn't ignore the results because, if you continue with your current lifestyle, you cannot take the tranquilisers I've prescribed for you because it could be extremely dangerous. They don't mix, I'm afraid, with the other drugs that you take.'

'I don't take any other drugs, apart from the odd paracetamol.' What is he talking about?

'Mia.' He leans forward over the desk and lowers his voice. 'I can assure you that whatever you tell me inside this room, stays inside this room. And, as a doctor, my duty is to help you, not to judge you. You can be completely honest with me.'

'I'm sorry,' I say. 'I have no idea what you're talking about.'

He sits back and frowns.

'I'll be frank with you, Mia. I'm talking about your drug use. "Recreational drugs" would be the term used now, I believe. Your blood and urine results show a heavy concentration of several different substances. I can tell you without a doubt that your use of recreational drugs is exacerbating, or even causing, your sleep problems as well as your confusion.'

19

Sebastian isn't happy; I can hear it in his voice, even though I can't see him.

'But I've booked a table; I thought you were feeling better.'

'I do, but I don't feel up to going out for dinner, Sebastian. You know how ill I've been. I'm just not up to sitting in a restaurant and making polite conversation.'

'Well then let me come round and look after you. I'll make us something really nice for dinner and then you'll feel a whole lot better.'

'Sorry. I just don't feel like it.' Which is the truth; I have the most appalling headache. But not all of the truth.

'I can cook you something delicious, I promise you.'

His voice is wheedling and I want to just hang up right now because I don't want him coming round.

Ever.

'Or you could come to mine,' he goes on. 'I could come and pick you up. It'll be a change of scenery for you, because you've spent days in your apartment. You must be sick of the sight of the place.'

'I'm going to bed in a minute.'

'It's six o'clock, Mia; you can't go to bed at six o'clock.'

'Well, I can,' I snap. 'Because I'm exhausted and I need to sleep and that's what I'm going to do. I'm going now, Sebastian. Goodnight.'

I press the button to end the call before he can answer and toss my phone onto the sofa.

I should have just been straight with him and told him we're over; I'm delaying the inevitable but I simply don't have the energy to have that conversation with him right now. I'm taking the cowards way out and putting it off because I can't face it at the moment.

I felt sick just talking to him, let alone seeing him.

Because I don't trust him any more.

What Doctor Campbell told me this morning

has shocked me to the core; how can I have been taking recreational drugs and not know that I'm doing so?

It's not possible, was my first thought. And then I realised that it's entirely possible if someone has been giving me drugs without me knowing. That would explain everything. I hold my head in my hands and try to think; my thoughts keep firing off at tangents and each time I think I've figured something out, the thought vanishes like smoke into thin air as I fail miserably to grasp hold of it. But there is one thing that I do remember and that I'm quite sure about; the last two episodes that I experienced started in the afternoon at work. I remember feeling fine when I arrived at work in the morning; it was only after lunch that I began to feel strange.

After Sebastian had made me a cup of coffee. I think Sebastian is drugging me.

What I don't understand is why. What possible reason could he have for doing that? I thought we were in a relationship; he seemed to genuinely like me and I liked him. I can't think of any reason for him to drug me. And then I remembered how concerned he was when I vanished from work: his phone calls and constant messaging.

Was he afraid he'd gone too far and given me too

much? Did he think I was going to die and he'd get found out?

There could have been times before that, too, but I can't remember with any clarity exactly what I was doing, or where I was, when I had the other episodes. My brain is so fuddled that I can't recall the circumstances but I know for sure that on the last two occasions at least, Sebastian was definitely with me before the episodes started.

I can't think of any possible reason for why he would do it – but does he need a reason? People do all sorts of things for all sorts of reasons; drinks get spiked all of the time in clubs and pubs. Maybe Sebastian gets off on doing it and likes having that power over me so he can then pretend to be concerned and play the doting boyfriend. Maybe it makes him feel needed. Maybe he's a psychopath or a sociopath because they don't go around with a label on their head, do they? He's personable and charming and aren't those psychopathic traits? He could be an axe-murderer for all I know because really, I don't know him very well. I only met him when I started working at the gallery which was less than a year ago. He's never really spoken very much about previous relationships. He's told me that he's never been serious with anyone because he had no intention of settling down until he was older. Is that suspicious? I don't know; I've never discussed exboyfriends with him either, because I could hardly tell him about Marco. My relationship with Marco was insular and very much under the radar. Apart from Carrie, no one knew we were together. I was secretive about him and kept him all to myself. I told myself this was because I didn't want to share him with anyone, but the truth was, Marco wasn't interested in being a 'proper couple'. I never met any of his friends and if I mentioned mine, he would sneer at their unearned wealth and make derogatory remarks despite never having met them. He'd ask why I bothered with them, when I had him. He didn't need anyone else so why did I?

I try to think back to when I stayed over at Sebastian's. I thought I slept well because I had no nightmares but what if that wasn't true? Maybe the rumour that Sebastian spiked someone's drink at the gallery was true; I assumed Tally made it up but what if she didn't? There's no smoke without fire. What if he'd drugged me with something that made me forget, a date-rape drug or something? It's perfectly possible. Whilst I was imagining I was sleeping soundly, I could have been unconscious and he could have been doing God knows what to me.

I shudder.

I try to think back over events since Sebastian and I started dating: his behaviour, his sexual habits. He's always been the perfect gentleman and a considerate and gentle lover.

But maybe he's not.

Maybe he's hiding his true self; that gentlemanly front could be hiding a brute of a man, for all I know. If he'd drugged me so that I wouldn't remember, I'd never know what he was really like. Who knows what might have happened when I stayed over because he has no flatmate to see what he was doing. I felt safer there, but it could have been the exact opposite and I was too doped up to know what had gone on. Carrie being here would have cramped his style, although when he did stay here, I didn't have any nightmares either because I remember being afraid of his witnessing them.

Unless he drugged me then, too.

A significant amount of recreational drugs: those were the words Doctor Campbell used. Amphetamines, cannabis, and other things that I've never even heard of. He didn't believe me, of course, when I said that I didn't take drugs and why would he when he has the evidence in front of him? He told me that it's not unusual for addicts to be in denial: to convince themselves that they don't take as many drugs as the think they do. *Much as a smoker is never as truthful about how many cigarettes they smoke,* he added with a smile.

How can I ever trust a man again after what I've discovered? I can't, is the short answer. Sebastian could have killed me; how was he to know how much to give me or how I would react? Even if the drugs themselves didn't kill me, I could easily have had an accident whilst under the influence of them. I could have been run over by a bus, fallen out of a window, God knows what else, because I was clearly hallucinating, so anything is possible. The only consolation in finding out about the drugs is that it means I'm not going mad, and that is such a massive relief. I truly believed that I was suffering from some sort of mental illness and I had no clue when, or if, an episode would strike again. I suppose that the fact that I'm not going mad, at least, is something to be grateful for.

I get up and wander out to the kitchen and fill myself a large glass of water and take a couple of paracetamol in the hope that they'll help my pounding head. I walk through into the bedroom, lie on top of the duvet and close my eyes. I think about taking a tranquiliser for all of ten seconds before deciding not to.

No more drugs; they're slowing my brain down and I need to work out what's going on. Logically, I know it must be Sebastian, but deep down, I still can't quite believe that he would do that to me.

* * *

It's dark when I awake and when I look at my phone, I see it's nearly ten o'clock.

My headache has gone but I have a sickly, hollow feeling in my stomach and I recognise it as hunger. I've barely eaten anything for the last few days but now I have an appetite. I'm starving. I get out of bed, pad out into the hallway and flick the light on. The apartment is so quiet that I don't need to look to know that Carrie isn't home yet. She seems to spend all of her life at work and I wonder how any job can be worth it. Although it's much different for her; unlike me, she has to work and doesn't have a choice.

I go into the kitchen, flick the light on and go straight over to the tap and fill the kettle. While it's heating, I pull open the fridge to see what there is to eat. A clingfilmed plate of cold pizza stares back at me: the leftovers from last night's takeaway. I didn't eat very much of mine and it looks significantly less appetising now than it did last night. I take one slice off the top, put it on a plate and set it heating in the microwave. I return the plate of pizza to the fridge and then stand and watch the turntable go around and wonder what I'm going to do. If only Carrie were here; I wouldn't need to be churning everything over and over in my head. I'm going to end up with another headache if I'm not careful. It would help me so much if Carrie and I could have a proper conversation, talk it all through and get it outside of my head. Get some perspective on it. I tell myself to stop being selfish but I can't help feeling disgruntled. I need you Carrie, and you're never here; you're always at bloody work.

The microwave dings and I take out the now nuclear-hot pizza. I stare at it for a moment and then walk over to the bin, open the lid and tip the plate over to one side and let the pizza slide into the bin. I can't face all that chewing and trying to get it down; just the thought of it makes me want to gag. A smoothie, that's what I'll have: nutritious and easy to swallow, absolutely no chewing involved. I go back to the fridge and pull open the door; two plastic containers of smoothies stand next to each other on the shelf and I take one out. My brain has been so fried that I don't even recall making them. It seems incredible that I've actually been capable of chopping and blending vegetables and fruit with the way I've been behaving over the last few weeks. Automatic pilot, I suppose. I walk over to the counter and take a glass down from the cupboard, pour the smoothie into it and put the container down when out of nowhere, the conversation with Jim pops into my head. I stand stock still and think about it, imagining myself standing in the foyer with him yesterday as he told me all about the email. The scattered thoughts that have been eluding and tormenting me begin to form themselves into cohesive thoughts, and with shocking clarity, I realise their significance.

Unsteady on my feet, I grip hold of the counter to steady myself. I stay this way until the dizziness eases and I feel steadier. I pick up the glass and stare at the thick, dark-green liquid for a moment and then pour it slowly down the sink.

20

I hear Carrie pottering around the kitchen as I walk down the hallway and it takes all of my will power not to turn around and go back to my room. I could pretend I'm ill, say I have yet another headache, but I'm not going to; I'm going to carry on walking and talk to my best friend in exactly the same way as I've always done.

'Morning!' She's at the counter buttering toast and looks refreshed and alert: everything that I don't feel. 'Want this?' She points at the toast with the knife. 'I can put some more in for me.'

'No, I'll have a coffee first, thanks.'

She shrugs and picks up a slice of toast and takes a bite. 'Did you sleep okay?'

I spoon coffee into a mug and flick the kettle on to boil.

I pull a face. 'Not really.'

'Oh God, not more nightmares?'

'No nightmares, just kept waking up. I had a really unsettled night.'

Mid-chew, she murmurs something I don't catch and I study her as she eats. Was she expecting me to have nightmares or am I going totally mad? Yesterday evening, I was convinced that Sebastian was trying to poison me and by the time I went to bed, I'd scrapped that idea and decided that it's my best friend who's the culprit. My oldest and dearest friend who's gone above and beyond what anyone should have to do for a friend. The best friend who has always had my back and has done far more for me than I've ever done for her. Part of me refuses to believe it, I don't want to believe it, but the seed of doubt has been sown. I keep asking myself, why? Why would Carrie try to poison me? It doesn't make any sense. I can't think of a single reason.

'Are you there?' Carrie's waving her hand in front of my face, laughing.

'Sorry?'

'You were miles away. I was saying, how do you fancy lunch at that trendy vegan place you love? We could have a route march round the big park first so we can stuff our faces guilt free afterwards, what do you think?'

'Sounds like a plan.'

'Great! I'll hit the shower because I have to wash my hair and you know how long that takes to dry.' She stuffs the last piece of toast into her mouth and heads out of the kitchen, munching as she goes. I watch her retreating back and wish that I hadn't remembered the conversation with Jim and what it meant, wish that I could banish it from my memory forever and go back to how things were.

But I can't; once you know something, you can't unknow it, however much you might want to.

Carrie admitted contacting head office and making the complaint against Owen; she said she did it because I told her Owen knew about Marco. She told me she reported him the day after I tried to view the video footage, when Owen was really off with me and said, 'I know what you did'.

But that was the *second* time she complained about Owen.

What Carrie *didn't* tell me was that she made two complaints against Owen.

When Jim told me about Owen, he said he'd had

a warning already about it and he hadn't heeded it, so was being dismissed. I didn't take much notice at the time but now it makes sense. When Owen said he knew what I did, he didn't mean Marco; he meant that he knew I'd made a complaint against him.

But it wasn't me, it was Carrie.

Why did she make the first complaint about him? She did that before I wrongly thought Owen knew about Marco, before he told me that he knew. There was no reason for her to complain about him because he hadn't done anything.

Why did she want Owen out of the way?

I could ask her; I should ask her and just get it out in the open. There could be a perfectly rational explanation, even though I've wracked my brains and can't think of a single one. But what if I have it all completely wrong? If I asked her to explain and she sees how I've doubted her, would she ever be able to forgive me?

Do I really want to risk ruining our friendship over a suspicion?

No, I don't.

Somehow, I have to find out the truth and put my mind at rest without her knowing. Other than Sebastian, she's the only other person who has the opportunity to poison me. Sebastian has access to my smoothies when I leave them in the fridge at work and he also definitely made me coffee when I had the last two episodes. Carrie has access to my food at home or she could have slipped something into a drink. I poured the smoothie away because I drink them almost every day but I honestly can't remember making any lately.

But I can't remember a lot of things.

The fact remains that someone is poisoning me and I need to find out who. But the biggest question of all and the one that I can't get my head around is, why? Why would Carrie do that? We've known each other since we were twelve, we're like sisters; we're more than sisters.

No, I can't believe she would do it, but to have any peace of mind at all, I need to prove that to myself.

Somehow.

* * *

We marched around the park, Carrie and I, arms linked, giggling and laughing as if everything was perfectly normal. We fed the ducks with some stale bread and we went to my favourite vegan café. I persuaded Carrie to try the falafel and yoghurt pittas –

she hates vegan food – and she admitted, begrudgingly, that she liked it. I told her it was okay to like it and it didn't mean that she had to turn full-on vegan because I hadn't either, but that it was another option, another choice of healthy food. We then had a huge slice of carrot cake because we'd earned it and because everything was so normal, I repeatedly had to ask myself if I'd imagined what Jim told me. I opened my mouth several times to ask her and then closed it again. How would I word it? *Carrie, are you poisoning me?*

We even talked about my penchant for having smoothies every day instead of proper food, how disgusted she is that my most favourite one, the one I eat more than any other is banana, orange and spinach. I studied her carefully as we were talking to see if she looked uncomfortable or as if she was lying.

She didn't.

She was the same Carrie that she's always been: funny, caring and absolutely on the same wavelength as me.

When we came back, she went off to get showered and changed because she's meeting some of her work colleagues for dinner tonight as one of them is retiring. I went off to my room as well because I told her I'm going out with Sebastian and needed to get ready.

But it was a blatant lie; I'm staying right here and when I'm quite sure Carrie has gone out and there's no possibility of her coming back, I'm going to search her room.

* * *

Nothing.

I've found absolutely nothing. Although I don't know exactly what I was looking for, I know that if I found a stash of drugs, that would have been damning evidence because Carrie doesn't do any sort of drugs. Paracetamol is about her limit and only when she absolutely has no choice. One of the rare occasions when we nearly fell out was when I got into using cocaine for a while on nights out; she was not happy about it.

So, no drugs and nothing else even slightly suspicious – but what did I expect? A note saying, 'I did it'?

I should be feeling better; I haven't found any evidence at all that Carrie has been drugging me. But that's the problem; I also haven't found anything to prove that she hasn't. All I've succeeded in doing is making myself feel like the absolute worst friend in the world for searching her best friend's room but despite that, I can't dispel the niggling doubt that I'm missing something. I stand in the middle of her bedroom and look around, making sure that I've put everything back exactly where I found it. And I must be a super sneaky, underhand person because I even had the foresight to take photographs of everything that I looked at to make sure I left it as I found it. Every drawer, the top of her dressing table, each shelf in her bathroom, even inside the bathroom cabinet; I photographed them all.

My phone shrills in my hand and I jump. I look down at the screen to see that it's Sebastian. It's the third time he's rung tonight. Yet again, I refuse the call and seriously consider blocking him. Seconds later, a message arrives.

Why aren't you answering? X

I should just finish with him instead of making the same feeble excuse of pretending to have a migraine. I'm not sure he believes me any more so why don't I just get it over with? My fingers hover over the keys but I can't bring myself to do it; it's cowardly and more to the point, I think he might turn up here if I tell him we're over. Which could be very bad.

Because either Carrie or Sebastian is poisoning me and I don't know who to trust.

I type him a message, hoping that he'll leave me alone.

Sorry, I was asleep. I'm so very exhausted and need to sleep. Will call you tomorrow X

He reads it immediately and I see he's typing back.

Okay. Get some rest and will speak tomorrow as I think we need to talk x

It sounds like I'm going to be the one who gets dumped. I think about it for a moment and then decide that it's too complicated to even think about now. How can I decide whether I care or not when I suspect him? I wander out of Carrie's bedroom and carefully close the door behind me, taking a last look around the room as I do so. I pad down to the lounge, turn on the TV and throw myself onto the sofa. I stare, unseeing, at the TV screen, as the sound of a Saturday-night gameshow washes over me. I pick up my phone and begin to idly scroll through Instagram. I rarely post anything but Suki pops up immediately with picture after picture of her new car. There's a picture of me, Suki, Imi, and Maria at the Diamond Lounge the last time we met up, but I don't remember the picture being taken. With a shock, I realise that I haven't seen them for weeks; we usually meet for lunch or drinks at least once a week but I don't remember even messaging them. I must have done so, but I can't remember.

I continue scrolling through and out of boredom, click on Carrie's profile. She bothers with social media even less than I do; she hasn't posted anything for months. I scroll through her feed and have gone back nearly a year when a picture catches my eye: it's a picture of the two of us grinning and raising a glass of champagne to the camera. It was taken at one of the first exhibitions I attended at the gallery and I'd taken Carrie along with me. I took the photograph and WhatsApped it to her but had no idea she'd posted it on Instagram. I study the picture and wish I could go back in time because I'd do a lot of things differently. I'd only just met Marco then; if I could have only seen the future, I'd have ditched him immediately before I got in too deep.

I scroll past and go further back onto Carrie's feed but aside from the odd picture of the two of us out clubbing, the only posts she has are reposts from other people and photos she's been tagged in. Before very long, I'm back to her university days and a younger, chubbier Carrie with long, dark hair appears, wearing slightly hippy-ish clothes. I scroll through, remembering this younger version of Carrie, and I feel nostalgic for our schooldays and then remember that in reality, they weren't that great until Carrie came along. I'm about to click out of her feed when I come to a post titled:

Third year and all ready to graduate!

Mortar-boarded and gowned, it's a group picture of Carrie's university graduation. I zoom in on Carrie standing at the front, a huge smile on her face. She was so proud of her first-class degree and I feel a pang of envy at her dedication; unlike me, once she starts something, she works hard and sticks at it until the end. I feel disgusted with myself for even thinking about doubting her and actually searching her room.

Really, Mia? This is how you treat your best friend?

I zoom out from the photo and am about to close the app when something catches my eye. I zoom in again and bring the phone closer, moving the photograph sideways so I can get a better look at the person standing behind Carrie.

The hair is covered by the mortar board but the lopsided smile, the dark, dangerous eyes are exactly the same.

It's Marco.

21

They knew each other.

All this time, they knew each other.

The knowledge bounces around my brain as the devastating truth hits me.

When Carrie was pretending to hate Marco when I first met him, she was lying; she'd known him for years. I take a deep, shuddering breath and try to think. I search my memory, desperately wanting to be wrong, but I know that I'm not; Carrie has lied to me continually since the day I met Marco. She pretended to me that he was a stranger, that she'd never met him before. She never once admitted that she knew him.

They set me up.

But why? What have they gained?

Twenty-five thousand pounds. I gave her twenty-five thousand pounds to get rid of the Marco problem, to get rid of his body after I'd killed him. Because Carrie did what she's always done: she sorted out my problem.

But there wasn't a problem.

With sudden, shocking clarity, I know with absolute certainty that Marco is still alive. They tricked me into believing I killed him to get money out of me.

I pace around the lounge, unable to keep still, horrified with what I've discovered but more than horror, I begin to feel anger: the kind of anger that I haven't felt for a long, long time.

Not since Gramma.

I want to smash something, do something to take this rage out of me. I look around the room for something to throw but I know that once I start, I'll be unable to stop; I'll smash the whole room up and still feel no better afterwards. I put my arms over my head and close my eyes and take several deep breaths to try and calm myself but all I can see is Carrie's face.

Her lying, cheating face.

How could she do this to me?

She's my best friend.

Was my best friend.

I trusted her more than I've ever trusted anyone in my life; I loved Carrie like a sister and she's betrayed me in the worst way possible, and for what?

A measly twenty-five thousand pounds.

If she'd asked, I would have given it to her. If she needed money so desperately, she only had to say the word and I would have gladly helped her. And why poison me? What did that achieve? She already had the money so why poison me and make me think I was going mad? Did she want to send me back to the same dark place I was in when Gramma died?

I drop onto the sofa and the anger begins to dissipate and I want to cry, because my best friend has betrayed me, and our friendship is over forever. There is no way back for us now because I'm not, and never have been, the forgiving type.

Carrie is dead to me now.

But that doesn't stop the grief.

I've lost my one and only true friend: the girl who I grew up alongside and shared so many moments with. The friend who's always looked after me and who, in my way, I looked after all those years ago when she started at my school as a scholarship girl. I protected her from the snobs and bullies and even though I did it because we were essentially the same

– two outcasts – I didn't have to do it. My life would have been so much easier then if I hadn't and even now, how many times have I defended her when others sneered and laughed at her? Too many times, too many to count.

I have many other friends, but they're not true friends, not like I thought Carrie was. They're good-time friends: people to go out partying and have fun with, fancy dinner companions, holiday friends. People who come from the same background as me, where money isn't a problem and to even talk about it is seen as coarse.

None of them are anything like the Carrie I thought I knew: loyal, steady, honest, kind-hearted and absolutely always there for me. I desperately want there to be an explanation for the photograph of Marco at university with her that means she didn't betray me, that she didn't set me up.

But there isn't one, however much I might wish there was. He's standing right behind her and there is no doubt they've both tricked me. Because Carrie knows me so well; she knew that I'd find Marco irresistible the first time I met him because so many of my boyfriends have been just like him. She knew I'd be hooked from the moment he behaved as if he wasn't interested in me. She knew that it would make him all the more desirable to me. I've always been drawn to the bad boy, the handsome man with a hint of danger about him who treats me badly. She knew all this, so when I met Marco – apparently by chance in a club – I was pretty much guaranteed to fall for him.

'Treat her mean and keep her keen.' That's what Carrie used to say about me when I got into yet another disastrous relationship. I remember how she was when I told her Sebastian had asked me out; I knew she didn't like him, but I thought she might approve because at least he was respectable and owned an art gallery. He was nothing like the unsuitable men that I usually got involved with, but maybe the real reason she didn't want me to start seeing him was in case he became suspicious of her. She wanted no witnesses to my strange, drug-induced behaviour. Poor Sebastian: how close he came to being blamed for everything. That's another thing I can't understand: drugging me. Does Carrie really hate me so much that she wanted to send me mad? She was there every night when I woke screaming from one of my nightmares; she witnessed the confusion and paranoia that I was fighting against almost daily. She saw the terror in me when I saw Marco on the camera footage from the door.

She saw and she didn't care; maybe she enjoyed it.

I see now that she simply deleted the footage from my phone before she woke me that day; she sat there and calmly deleted it whilst I was dozing, and then convinced me that I'd imagined ever seeing it. That's why he came here; his visit and capture on camera were solely to make me think I was losing my mind.

How could they be so cruel?

And where was it going to end?

A sudden thought strikes me, and I go out into the kitchen and pull open the fridge. There are two of my smoothie containers on the shelf, both full.

Yesterday, I tipped one away but now there are two.

That explains why I don't remember making them; I didn't, Carrie did. She's been making them and putting them in exactly the same place I always put them to make me think that I'd put them there. I reach in and take one in each hand and walk over to the sink, intent on tipping them all away. I stop and put them down on the counter and stare at them.

Think, Mia, think.

If I tip them away, she'll know that I've found her out.

I pick them up and carry them back to the fridge. I don't want to make her suspicious or give her any inkling that I know what she's been doing.

Let her think their plan is working.

Whatever their plan is.

I tell myself not to be melodramatic, but I can't help thinking the worst.

What if they're trying to kill me?

* * *

Carrie didn't come home until one o'clock this morning. I heard the front door open and her walking to her room even though my bedroom door was firmly closed because I was lying awake in bed, unable to sleep There's no doubt in my mind that the story about a work colleague retiring was a lie and that really, she's been with Marco. All the times that she was working late, all the excuses about the places she's been, she'll have been with him.

I get up at eight o'clock after a sleepless night and head into the kitchen, checking as I go past that her bedroom door is closed. I take one of the smoothies out of the fridge, tip it into a glass and then tip it down the plughole, running the tap afterwards to make sure every trace of it has gone. I leave the container and glass next to the sink so that Carrie will see them and assume that I've drunk it.

I put the kettle on, turn on the radio and hope that the noise reaches her room. Carrie isn't one for lying in bed; she's always up by eight thirty, even on weekends, because she's a creature of habit. If she sticks to her routine, she'll be in here very shortly to eat her breakfast, drink a cup of coffee and then go back to her en suite to shower.

And while she's in the shower, I can look at her phone.

I make myself a coffee and sit down at the breakfast bar and wait. At twenty-five past eight, she walks into the kitchen and looks at me in surprise.

'Wow, you're up early! I thought you were staying over at Sebastian's?'

'No, that's tonight,' I lie. 'We're going out with some friends of his and it's going to be a late one, so I'll crash at his. How was your meal last night?'

She pulls a face. 'Boring. Tedious. Almost as dull as work but at least there was a free meal in it. Do you want toast?' She holds up the loaf of bread.

'No thanks, I've had a smoothie. I'm eating out tonight so I needed to counteract that with something healthy.'

'Yuk. Rather you than me.'

She turns and drops two slices of toast into the toaster and I think what a good actress she is: what a convincing and consummate liar. She must hate me so much. I watch as she takes the butter from the fridge and bustles around in her normal morning way and think how sad it is that our friendship is over. She sits down at the breakfast bar opposite me and I sip my coffee.

'No eligible men there, then?' I ask.

'God, no,' she says with a laugh. 'I should be so lucky.'

Was that a flicker of guilt there? There was definitely something, or perhaps I'm imagining it. Carrie hasn't had many boyfriends and the few she's had were serious accountant types who lasted mere weeks before she tired of them. None of them ever stayed the night here and she never seemed really into them and for a while, I wondered if she might be gay. I never asked her, despite believing we were best friends, because not everything has to be shared. I assumed if she wanted me to know, she would tell me. I have my secrets, too. Secrets that I've never, and will never, tell. Who she sees doesn't matter to me one way or the other, but I thought maybe it mattered to her, maybe she was private about her sexuality, because some people are. And then after a while,

I stopped wondering because she never really talked about men or women or relationships, because her life was about work, work, work, and getting on in her career.

Or so I thought.

'Better get a move on,' she says, standing up and carrying her plate over to the sink. 'Jean, the retiree, has invited us all to her house for a little soiree, as she calls it, as if last night wasn't bad enough. Wish I could get out of it, but it'll look bad if I don't turn up. It'll be a beige buffet on paper doilies and sparkling white wine in her best fancy wine glasses. Awful. What a way to spend a Sunday afternoon.'

I laugh and she heads off out of the kitchen towards her bedroom and I hear the door close. I wait a few minutes and then go out into the hallway and stand outside her door. I move closer, put my ear against it and listen. I hear movement and then the sound of a door being closed, and I guess she's gone into her en suite. Taking a deep, steadying breath, I take hold of the handle, slowly lower it and gently push the door open.

I can hear the sound of the shower running and I look around the room for her phone. It's sitting on top of the dresser and I step quickly towards it and pick it up. I punch in her date of birth and pray that she hasn't changed the code. I heave a sigh of relief when the screen unlocks and I scroll quickly to her WhatsApp messages and open them.

It opens on a conversation with M.

Obviously Marco.

I quickly read the page of messages, listening to make sure she's still in the shower.

> Carrie: Last night was great! Such a shame I couldn't stay the night x

> M: It won't be for much longer x

> Carrie: I know but it seems to be taking for-ever x

> M: Patience, remember? See you this after-noon. Don't be late, I've got a present for you x

> Carrie: love you x

I feel the bile rise in my throat as I read; he sounds nothing like the Marco I knew. Marco rarely bothered to respond to my messages, let alone buy me any presents. As I recall, I picked up the bill whenever we went out anywhere. But it's different now; they have my twenty-five thousand pounds to splash around. When I think back over the few months I was with Marco, I paid for pretty much everything and let him treat me like crap and I wonder why I thought that was acceptable. And how did Carrie feel about him having sex with me? He certainly couldn't fake that; sex was the only power I had over him because he couldn't get enough of me.

Maybe I'll tell Carrie that because I'm sure Marco won't have.

Rage courses through me again and I want to hurl the phone across the room or smash it onto the top of the dresser until it's shattered into a thousand pieces. A vision of myself storming into the bathroom and dragging Carrie out of the shower by her hair, the shock on her face, her surprise that I know exactly what she's been doing to me, flashes through my mind. I enjoy the thought for a moment; confident that I will have my revenge on both of them, somehow.

But not yet.

The sound of running water has stopped and Carrie will walk out of that bathroom at any moment. I quickly replace the phone where I found it, hurry to the bedroom door and let myself out, pulling it silently closed behind me.

I stand in the hallway and think about what I've just read and then head towards my room. Time to get showered and dressed.

I'm going out.

22

I shower and get dressed as quickly as possible. I couldn't decide what to wear and managed to make a simple, everyday process unnecessarily drawn out. Why does it matter what I wear after what I've discovered? Only it does; it matters a lot. I want to look good for myself: much better than Carrie. Even though common sense tells me that I always look better than her – not conceit, just the truth – if I can believe those text messages, then there's no denying that Marco still chose her over me.

Dull, dependable, the fun sponge, the book-keeper, scholarship girl, Carrie.

Not my words but others'. Sebastian's for a start but as well as him, many other people didn't like

Carrie and had the same opinion of her. Most of the girls at school disliked her because she was a scholarship girl but also because she was so different to them: she didn't fit in, but more than that, she made no attempt to. She didn't endear herself to people or try to make them like her. The few that did try to befriend her, apart from me, were the geeks and the unpopulars, but even they gave up after a while when they were met with indifference. She did nothing to make herself likeable and it's only because I was persistent that we became friends. I mistook her aloofness and seriousness for trustworthiness and loyalty. Eventually, I won her over through sheer determination and felt pleased with myself because I'd made her my friend and everyone else had failed. I now see that she allowed me in because I was useful: rich and eager to please.

Carrie has always done exactly as she wanted and refused to adapt to fit in with others; refused to bend, to change her ways or join the herd. She was at school to get an education and nothing was going to get in her way; she simply didn't, and doesn't, need other people. When Gramma called her cold and rude, I defended her. I told Gramma that Carrie hadn't had the benefit of an upbringing like ours; that she hadn't been taught any manners and didn't know how to behave. Gramma was an awful snob and she didn't like Carrie because she came from a poor background. But perhaps it was more than that; maybe she saw her for what she was.

I always defended her. Always.

But no more.

Once I'd broken down Carrie's barriers, she looked after me and became my most loyal and trusted friend, or so I thought.

Not any more.

I zip up my jeans and study myself in the mirror: lemon, crop jeans, white, cotton top and my hair hanging loosely around my face.

I look good, heck – better than good – but I'm nervous.

I stand still for a moment and listen; Carrie won't go out without saying goodbye so she must still be here. Maybe she's in her bedroom; maybe she's texting her lover. My insides twist as I imagine them together, but I'm not sure whether it's because of Carrie or Marco.

Maybe it's both. A double betrayal. The both of them plotting against me and laughing at my naivety and gullibility. Their confidence that they could take twenty-five thousand pounds from me and I would have no idea I was being conned. I push down the rage and remind myself that anger achieves nothing; revenge is much sweeter. Carrie will be going out soon to meet him and I'm going to follow her. What I'm going to do when I see them together, I'm not sure; I haven't planned that far ahead.

I'll see what happens.

I open the bedroom door, step into the hallway and walk down to the kitchen. Carrie's bedroom door is still closed but she'll have to come out soon to go the fictional work 'soiree'. I linger in the kitchen and wait; I need to be able to follow her as soon as she's left the apartment but obviously, I don't want her to see me. I hear her bedroom door open so I quickly turn to the sink and begin to wash the smoothie container so it looks as if I'm doing something.

'You look nice.'

I turn and smile at her words and I see her eyes settle briefly on the smoothie container. She'll be expecting me to have another episode soon because she believes I drank it for breakfast.

'Ditto,' I say, with a smile. 'Love your dress.' She's wearing a white and pink, flowery, halter-neck summer dress with white strappy wedges. I realise that she's been make more of an effort with her appearance lately and wonder that I never noticed this before.

The intercom shrills loudly and I jump. The container falls into the sink with a clatter.

'God, Mia, are you okay?' Carrie looks at me with fake concern and I make myself look worried and don't answer. She thinks the smoothie is kicking in. She presses the intercom button and I hear Jim saying that Sebastian is here and before I can stop her, Carrie tells Jim to send him up.

'You did know he was coming, didn't you?' She bites her lip as if she's done something wrong and for a second, I wonder if she knows what I had planned; if somehow, she knows I've found her out. 'I assumed he was picking you up?'

'Yes, he is,' I lie.

The doorbell buzzes and I go out to let him in. Carrie follows me. As I open the door to him, she squeezes past him with a cheery 'See you later,' to me and is gone, and with her, my chance of following her. She makes no attempt to acknowledge Sebastian and it strikes me that she's offhand like that with a lot of people and does little to endear herself to anyone. Why did I like her so much and think she was such a great person?

'Mia.' Sebastian leans down and kisses me on the cheek in a cloud of expensive aftershave. 'How are you?'

'Fine.' I head into the kitchen. 'Coffee?' I call over my shoulder.

He follows and sits down on a stool at the breakfast bar, his long legs stretched out in front of him. I feel him watching me as I take two mugs out the cupboard and take the milk out of the fridge.

'Instant or the proper stuff? I can do either.'

'Whatever's easiest.'

I spoon coffee into mugs and wait for the kettle to boil.

'So you're feeling better, now?' Sebastian asks. 'Migraine all gone?'

'Yes, much better. I feel like my old self again.' The kettle boils and I make the coffee, splash some milk in and carry the cups to the breakfast bar.

'Biscuit?' I ask.

'No thanks. Mia, can you sit down? I need to talk to you.'

I pull out a stool opposite him, perch on it and try not to feel annoyed. As I suspected, he's come round here to finish with me and in the process, has ruined my chance to follow Carrie and catch her with Marco. I know that Marco is alive, but I need to see the bastard with my own eyes.

Sebastian could have just messaged me, couldn't he? Most men would take the easy way out and do the dumping via text; it's much less embarrassing that way. I would have preferred it because there's nothing else to be said once you've made the decision to finish with someone. As far as I'm concerned, there's no going back. I wouldn't humiliate myself by begging him to reconsider and let's not forget that I thought he was poisoning me. That hardly bodes well for a relationship, does it? I thought so little of him that I believed he could do something like that. We haven't been seeing each other for very long either, so it's not as if I'm going to break down and be heartbroken. This is so typical of well-brought up Sebastian; he has to do the right thing and be the gentleman about it and if it wasn't for his timing, I'd think it was quite sweet. The sort of men I usually go for aren't well-mannered or in any way nice and when we finish, it's by having a screaming row or one ghosting the other until they tire of trying and melt away.

'Mia?'

Sebastian is studying my face and I realise I was miles away.

'Sorry. What was it you wanted to talk about?'

'Us. Me and you.'

I wait, irritation rising. *I'm really not bothered*, I want to say, to let him off the hook because he looks quite anxious, and he really needn't be. But that would be a bit insulting if I said that, wouldn't it? I am a bit surprised that it's obviously bothering him because I've not seen this side of Sebastian before; he's always cool and laid back.

'So...' He looks uncomfortable. 'This last week when you've been ill has made me think about things. And the thing is...' He pauses and I stare at him, willing him to say the words and get it over with so he can leave. He looks down at his hands for a moment and then looks up and stares straight into my eyes. 'The thing is, Mia, I've fallen in love with you.'

* * *

I lie in bed and luxuriate in the feel of the silk sheets against my skin and the softest pillows ever. We're in Sebastian's bed and I have to admit that his bed linen is top notch. Much better than mine. I think I'm going to replace all of my bedding once I've got rid of Carrie; I'll give my apartment a bit of a makeover. Perhaps get the decorators in, give the whole place a brand-new look, change the furniture; it's not as if I can't afford it. It'll give me something to concentrate on and take my mind off the massive betrayal by my best friend.

Sebastian is pottering around in the kitchen rustling up a snack for us and I relax and think back on the day. I didn't tell him I loved him back; I said I really liked him but it was too soon for me, but who knows? I could see he was disappointed but I assured him that I've never felt so close to anyone before, so I think that made him feel a bit better. I was fully intending to finish with him, despite his declaration of love, but it suddenly struck me that being with Sebastian could be a good thing. It could be useful. We've spent a very nice day together and I'm staying here for the night. I've put the Carrie problem to one side for now because I'm going to have to give it some serious and proper thought. I don't want to go steaming in and doing something that I'm going to regret later. I'm thinking things through carefully to decide what action I'll take.

Sebastian and I went to a lovely little bistro for Sunday lunch and afterwards, we went for a riverside stroll in Little Venice. It was stunning: cute boats and pretty scenery, made all the prettier by the sunshine and warmth. We walked around for hours and it's such a lovely place that I'm astounded I've never been there before. It was quite romantic too; Sebastian held my hand the whole time and only let go of it when we had to get into his car. He kept glancing at me and smiling and was so sweet.

If slightly boring.

But no matter; I managed not to think about Carrie and Marco for quite long periods of time and that's the main thing. After our walk, we came back here and of course we tumbled into bed because we had to celebrate our new status as a proper couple, even though I haven't said the L-word yet. And it was very enjoyable, both times, and did me the power of good because this week has been extremely tense and I had a lot of bottled up tension to get rid of. I felt a lot better afterwards and have managed to banish the thoughts of Sebastian being a psychopath and drugging me senseless. I'm fortunate that I have the ability to not dwell on the past and pine for what might have been or wish that things were different; I just get on with things and move on.

'Scrambled eggs okay?' Sebastian appears in the bedroom doorway with a tray, wearing only a blue-striped apron tied around his waist. He should look ridiculous but doesn't, he looks super-hot and I feel a stirring of lust. He's not my usual type but he is very attractive and there's a lot to be said for that.

'Fabulous.' I smile my approval, pull myself up onto the pillows and drag the duvet up to my armpits.

He lowers the tray onto my lap and then sits on the edge of the bed next to me. There are two platefuls of scrambled egg, each with a slice of toast cut into perfect triangles on the side. Sebastian will make someone the perfect husband.

'I've really enjoyed today.'

'Me too,' I say. And truthfully, I have. Sebastian has the been the perfect antidote to the Carrie problem; today has been fun and enjoyable and just what I needed. The upside to finding out that Carrie is a cheating, lying bitch is that, without a doubt, I am not going mad; my mental health is perfectly fine. I no longer fear that I'll end up in the same place as I did after Gramma died. My overactive brain has calmed down and now, when Carrie and Marco pop into my head, I'm able to remain calm. If any anger bubbled up, I told myself to channel that rage into planning what I'm going to do about them and how I'm going to have my revenge.

And the good thing is, it worked.

Because now, I have a plan.

23

Tally has been prowling around the gallery this morning, obviously bored and wanting someone to talk to. She wanders over to me and I chat to her for a while – pretty impossible not to as she's perched on the edge of my desk – and I drop into the conversation that Carrie is moving in with her boyfriend and I'm helping her with her packing tonight.

'Ooh, are you looking for a new flatmate? I hate it where I live and I'd love to move in with you because we get on so well,' she says with a hopeful look on her face. Even if I wanted a flatmate – which I absolutely do not – Tally is the last person I'd choose; she's far too loud and overbearing. I'll be living alone once Carrie has gone because I never wanted a flatmate in the first place. I only allowed Carrie to live with me because she was my best friend and I knew she'd never be able to afford anywhere decent on her own.

'Well.' I lean closer and drop my voice an octave as if I'm imparting a great secret. 'I'd love you as a flatmate but I just don't think Carrie will be staying with him for very long because he's a bit controlling. I think a few weeks of him and she'll want to move right back in with me.'

Her eyes light up at the prospect of a bit of gossip and after looking around to make her think I'm checking to make sure we're not overheard, I ply her with more details.

'He's so weird: doesn't like her having friends or seeing anyone, not even me.' I plaster a shocked look on my face. 'And he's peculiar about the people she works with. Her work colleagues, quite honestly, are all about a hundred years old and as dull as ditchwater, but he thinks she's going to have an affair and leave him or something. I mean how ridiculous, being jealous of work colleagues? Although I get the feeling Carrie sort of likes it in a way because she thinks it means he loves her. I've tried to tell her it's not a good thing and it's most definitely not flattering, but she refuses to listen. I think she knows deep down that it's not right because they've finished a few times over it, but he always persuades her to go back to him. He swears undying love and promises to change but it never works, does it? Because people don't change; they are what they are.'

Tally frowns and blows air out through pursed lips. 'She needs to get rid, as soon as, because he'll only get worse. I've been with someone like that and I can tell you it was no fun. Before you know it, you don't have any friends and they're running your life and checking your phone. Is Carrie the one who comes to the openings with you sometimes? Mousy hair, bit old-fashioned looking?'

'Yes, that's her.'

Tally shakes her head. 'No offence, Mia, but she's a bit drab, isn't she? I'm shocked that she's gone for someone like that, because she looks the sensible type.'

'I think that's the trouble; she's not really had a lot of luck with men and she's mistaking possessiveness for love. She's not interested in fashion or overly bothered what she wears but he even has a lot to say about that: doesn't like her showing any leg or the slightest hint of sexiness. Wants her to dress like a librarian. She's my best friend and I love her to bits, but I just can't seem to get through to her. Sadly, she's going to have to move in with him and learn the hard way. But on the upside, at least she'll have her old room to come back to when she's had enough of him.'

'You're a good friend, Mia; not many people would do that for her.'

I shrug. 'We've known each other a long time and we've got each other's backs; that's just how it is.'

'He must have something going for him to attract her in the first place, though, mustn't he? What's he like?'

I frown and look thoughtful.

'A bit strange, although obviously I've never said that to Carrie. He's quite good-looking in a brooding sort of way but not great at conversation. Carrie actually met him when were on a night out together. We were in a club and he hit on me first and when I didn't want to know, moved onto Carrie.'

'Noooo!' Tally looks shocked, and also delighted, and I realise that I'm rather enjoying myself. 'And it doesn't bother her that she was second best?' she probes.

I bite my lip and affect an uncomfortable look.

'What? Do tell!' Tally leans closer.

'It's weird, because she was there; she saw him attempting to chat me up. Obviously, I wasn't in the slightest bit interested because I knew he was a bit odd, straight off the bat. You can just tell, can't you? Something not quite right about him: a bit too intense. He asked me to dance and then wanted to buy me a drink and I said no to both and he didn't like it one little bit. Got a bit stroppy and asked me "why not?" and then called me stuck-up. I walked off to the ladies in the end, to get away from him.'

'And she saw all this?'

'Yep. The whole thing. But when I got back from the loo, she was making out with him. And when she told me she was seeing him, she behaved as if I'd never seen him before in my life. Told me she knew him from uni and that they'd always had an attraction to each other but had never acted on it. But honestly, Tally, when he hit on me, he hadn't even noticed her. Not so much as a first, let alone a second glance. She made out they locked eyes across the crowded club and just clicked, but the truth is, she was standing right next to me all night and he never even noticed her.'

Tally shakes her head in disbelief.

'I think that's why he never comes to the flat if I'm there, because he tried to chat me up first even though they both pretend it never happened. I often wonder if he got with Carrie as some sort of warped revenge for me giving him the brush off.'

'I wouldn't be surprised. I almost feel sorry for your friend because you know it's not going to end well for her.'

'No, it's not,' I say sadly.

Or him. It's not going to end well for either of them.

* * *

'I'll see you tomorrow.' I stand on tiptoes and kiss Sebastian briefly on the lips. He pulls me closer and the chaste kiss begins to turn into something much more.

'Anyone could walk in here,' I whisper, as we come up for air.

'I could lock the door,' Sebastian murmurs in my ear.

'No!' I pull away with a laugh. 'I have to go. Lots to do tonight.'

'Oh, yes, the fun sponge is moving out.'

'Sebastian.' I frown. 'You're not to call her that.'

He shrugs and then laughs.

'I'm just jealous that she gets to spend the evening with you tonight and I don't.'

'It's just one night,' I say. 'I couldn't exactly say no, could I?'

I've told Sebastian the same lie that I told Tally: that I'm helping Carrie pack her things ready to move.

'I suppose not. On the plus side, at least we'll be able to have some proper alone time at yours without her listening at the door.'

'Sebastian! Don't be so disgusting. She wouldn't do that.'

He grins. 'I was joking. I'm still getting over the shock that she actually has a boyfriend. I didn't think she had it in her. Can't imagine her kissing anyone, let alone having sex with them. I always assumed she'd die a virgin.'

'Don't be horrible,' I say, pretending I care. He has no idea that I now hate Carrie as much as I used to love her, that hearing him say snide things about her pleases me. *Go on, Sebastian: tell me exactly what you think of my soon-to-be ex-flatmate and don't mince your words.*

'I'm only being honest. From a man's viewpoint, she's got nothing going for her: miserable and frumpy, with a massive, working-class chip on her shoulder. What's to like?'

'I thought you were getting on okay with her now.'

'Only for your sake. Anyway, she likes me about as much as I like her.'

'Well I'm just worried, that's all. This boyfriend of hers is controlling and it's not healthy. I wish she wasn't moving in with him.'

'I wouldn't worry; it's him you want to feel sorry for.'

'I hope you're right. Anyway, I'm going now or else we'll never get it all done.' I pull on my jacket and loop my handbag over my shoulder. 'I'll see you tomorrow.'

He rushes to open the door for me – ever the gentleman – and I head out of his office, through the gallery and out onto the street and start walking in the direction of home. I march along but once I'm around the corner and out of sight of the gallery, I take my mobile phone out of my bag and order a cab. I'm not going home yet; the cab is to take me to Marco's flat because it struck me last night that he's probably still living there. Neither he nor Carrie would be worried about me turning up because they think I truly believe that I killed Marco there. I'd hardly be likely to revisit the scene of my crime. If he's moved, I'll need to revise my plan and find out where he lives, but I think he'll be there, because why would he go to the bother of moving somewhere else when he doesn't need to?

The cab arrives and I jump in. During the fifteen-minute journey, I think about what I'm going to do when I arrive. Am I going to knock on the door and confront them? Realistically, to prove to myself that Marco is still there, that's what I'm going to have to do. It'll be letting them know that *I* know what they've been up to, but that doesn't matter, because Carrie will be moving out of my flat tonight, with or without her belongings.

But I won't be helping her to pack; I might launch all of her clothes and belongings out of the window, but I definitely won't be helping her package them up all neat and tidy.

Far too quickly, we arrive in front of the ugly, seventies-built, grey, pebbledash apartment block where Marco lives. I tell the driver to pull up around the corner into the next street and after tutting at me and pulling a face, he does as I ask. Just for that, I don't give him a tip. As he drives off, I stand on the pavement to decide what I'm going to do.

I'll have to knock on his door; there's no other way to find out if he's still there. Carrie may even be in there with him instead of working late like she always pretends. I bet she never works late.

I feel a moment of unease. My ex-best friend and ex-boyfriend have been poisoning me; is it really wise to confront them? No one knows that I'm here; I could disappear and there would be no clue as to where I'd gone. Carrie on her own wouldn't be a problem but two of them is a different thing entirely; I'd be outnumbered.

Or am I being melodramatic?

I walk along the street and get to the corner, still undecided as to whether I'm going to confront them or not, when I stop dead in my tracks and slowly back up.

Carrie and Marco have just come out of the building entrance and are walking slowly down the path to the pavement, deep in conversation. I knew that Marco was alive but actually seeing him is still a shock. I take a few deep breaths to steady myself as the scale of the betrayal sinks in. I wish I hadn't come here now because if they turn, or even glance in this direction, they'll see me immediately. I look wildly around; there is nowhere to hide. Terraced houses line both sides of the street, their front doors opening straight out onto the pavement. There are no convenient back alleys or gardens I can hide in.

Nowhere.

I could squat behind a parked car but if they choose to walk down this street, they'll see me. I feel real fear as it dawns on me that I've put myself in a dangerous position. The relief is immense as I watch them turn in the opposite direction when they reach the pavement. How stupid was I to think I'd confront them both? I could have been playing right into their hands. Because if they're prepared to drug me, what else are they capable of? I pull out my phone to call a cab but also to do something else.

I need a locksmith.

Because Carrie is moving out tonight.

And I'm making sure she can never get back in.

24

It's amazing how quickly a locksmith will turn up if you pay them enough.

I'd hardly got home before Jim buzzed through from reception to say that there was a man to see me. It was Kez, the locksmith, and as he deftly replaced my lock with a brand spanking new one, he regaled me with some very witty stories of customers who had accidentally locked themselves out. I think they were embellished for effect but they were very funny and as I laughed, I felt almost light-hearted. Carrie will be leaving tonight and she won't be coming back; I'll be rid of my backstabbing ex-best friend forever. When Kez had finished, he gave me the shiny new keys – three of them – but didn't appear to be in any hurry to leave. He was clearly hoping for the offer of a cup of tea and whereas normally I would oblige, I wanted him gone just in case Carrie decided to come home early, unlikely though it was. I had to drop a couple of massive hints that my boyfriend was picking me up at any moment before he reluctantly packed up his tools and bid me goodbye. I gave him a very healthy tip on top of the extortionate fee, so I think that helped him forgive me for not making him a drink.

But now he's gone and I can't settle. I regret getting rid of him so quickly because at least he was a distraction. How long is Carrie going to be? She'll definitely be home at some point, but the question is, when? She never stays out all night as that would be a little hard to pass off as working late, but on occasion, she's come home as late as ten o'clock and still spun the yarn that she was working, so it could be a long wait. It's now eight thirty and despite not wanting to help her pack up her belongings, I go into the kitchen and rummage around in the cupboard underneath the sink and feel elated when I find a roll of dustbin bags. I take them into her room, shake one open and lay it on the carpet. I'm sure she has a suitcase somewhere so I'll leave the wardrobe to her, but the smaller stuff can go into bin bags. I walk over to the dressing table and pull open the top drawer to see underwear neatly laid out. I give the drawer a sharp tug and it comes completely out of the runners in my hands. I carry it over to the bin bag, upend it and tip the entire contents into the bag.

It's incredibly satisfying; so satisfying that I repeat the process with each drawer, filling a new bin bag each time. As I'm about to upend the final drawer into a bag, several sheets of paper tumble out of the mixture of odd socks and washed-out t-shirts. It's a bank statement. I pick it up, sit down on the bed and study it to discover another lie; she's always told me that her job is poorly paid and her salary won't improve until she's worked her way up the hierarchy.

Another lie.

She's very well paid; she earns more than twice as much as me. She's lived here rent free for years and made me afraid to even mention money, and all the time she's been earning a very healthy salary. I rip the statement into pieces, toss it into the bag and tip the rest of the contents after it. I get up and go into the bathroom, open the doors of the wall cabinet and study the contents for a moment before sweeping everything off the shelves and straight into a bag. A few bottles clatter a bit and I think there might be a few breakages as they tumbled in but I'm not worried. The plastic bag will contain any drips and pieces of glass. I tie the top into a knot and just to make sure none of it drips out of the bag onto my carpet, I walk into the bedroom and put the entire bag inside the bin bag containing her underwear. I wrap all of her underwear around it, giving it a good press in the process. There: her hideous, sensible knickers and bras will mop up any drips. I'm enjoying myself so much that it doesn't register at first that someone is pounding on the front door. Quite loudly, too.

I toss the underwear bag into the pile with the others, saunter out into the hallway and listen for a moment. The pounding is louder out here and someone is shouting, too. Carrie is loudly calling my name and asking me if I'm okay. I smile as I walk to the front door; she thinks I'm having one of my episodes again and is pretending to be concerned. I pull open the front door.

'Sorry,' I say, with a smile. 'I couldn't hear you.'

'Are you okay?' There's concern on her face: fake, obviously. 'What's wrong with the door?'

She steps inside and I close the door behind her.

'I had a new lock fitted.'

'A new lock? Why?'

'To keep you out.'

'What?' She stares at me in confusion, her eyes wide.

'To keep you out. You're moving out tonight and I had the locks changed to stop you from ever getting back in.'

'Are you feeling okay, Mia?' She puts her hand on my arm. 'Shall we go and sit down and talk about things? You know you've been a bit all over the place lately and getting the wrong idea sometimes.'

I slowly look down at her hand and then up at her face.

'Take your fucking hand off me, Carrie.'

Her mouth drops open in shock; I rarely swear and never at her.

She opens her mouth to speak but I hold my hand up to prevent her.

'I've started packing your stuff up for you in bin bags and I haven't been very careful so, if you don't want everything ruined, I suggest you go and do the rest yourself.'

Her mouth gapes and she looks a bit like a fish but I can see the tiniest flicker of comprehension dawning.

'Yes,' I say. 'I know what you've been doing to me. I know that Marco isn't dead. I know you tricked me out of twenty-five thousand pounds. I know everything, Carrie. You're leaving tonight and never coming back and I never want to see you again.' I turn my back to her and march off to her bedroom, pick up another bin bag, open it and give it a shake and look around to see what else I can put in it. Carrie appears in the doorway, staring open-mouthed at the bags lying around the room.

'What are you doing? You can't do that; that's my stuff.' She crosses to the bags, unties one and looks inside.

'I can do what I like; this is my apartment.'

'You bitch.' She glares at me.

Even though I know what she's done, I'm still shocked at the venom in her voice.

'That's a bit rich, coming from someone who's tricked me into believing I murdered my boyfriend and then proceeded to poison me.'

'I can't help it if you're thick, can I?' She laughs nastily. 'I mean, honestly, you thought I got someone off the dark web to dispose of Marco's body? Come on. Who'd believe something as far-fetched as that unless they're totally stupid? I almost felt pity for you then for being so completely gullible. Almost, but not quite; mostly, I found it hilarious, as did Marco.' All pretence has gone now; the true Carrie revealed for the first time ever. I'm shocked at the speed with which she's dropped the pretence that she was my friend; I thought it would take much longer.

'And you never even twigged about Owen,' she goes on. 'Even when he came round here and spelt it out for you. I mean, the only reason he had to go was because he'd seen Marco coming here, after he was supposedly dead. We couldn't risk him saying something to you, because you always had to talk to him, didn't you? To prove what a great person you are even though you're filthy rich. Even with blatant reg flags practically wagging in your face, you still never suspected. It was all there in front of you and you only had to put two and two together, but you're so dumb, you still couldn't work it out.'

'That's because I thought you were my friend, Carrie, my best friend. I trusted you. It never crossed my mind that you could do something like that.'

She throws the bag she's holding to the floor and storms towards me and for a moment, I think she's going to hit me. It flashes through my mind that I hope she doesn't; not because I'm afraid of her, but because once I hit her back, I'll be unable to stop.

She stops inches from me and I see her ball her hands into fists and hold them by her side.

'Friend?' she spits out the words. 'You don't know the meaning of the word. You're not my friend and you never have been. You're a rich bitch who thinks she can buy everything, including people. The truth is, Mia, I hate you and everything you stand for. I've always hated you.'

Of course she does, what did I expect her to say? But it's still staggering to see this side of Carrie that I've never witnessed before and it'll take some adjusting to. I honestly didn't think she had it in her.

'What I don't understand is why, Carrie, why do you hate me so much after all I've done for you? Without me, you wouldn't have lasted five minutes at Revensfield. Everyone was ready to make life difficult for you before they even met you because you were a scholarship girl. And you never exactly did anything to endear yourself to anyone, did you? Not even me, to start with. I protected you and, if it wasn't for me, you wouldn't have survived, scholarship or not.'

She laughs great hoots of laughter and I wonder if she's gone mad.

'You're so fucking deluded.' She's suddenly serious. 'Do you really think I ever liked you? You were useful, Mia. Useful. And I'd have managed just fine without you because, unlike you, I'm not a weak, flaky, self-entitled, spoilt brat who wants everyone to love me. I didn't care if everyone hated me, especially the spoilt bitches at that school. I don't actually give a shit what anyone thinks of me. I've had to be strong because I had nothing but a shit family who I couldn't wait to jettison. I tolerated your whining about being an orphan and your miserable granny and "poor you", because I got to live here for free, you thick cow.'

Even though I know what she and Marco have done, on some level, I'm still struggling to believe that it's come to this. Surely the last fourteen years can't all have been a lie? They can't have.

And yet they are.

I realise that I wasn't expecting this from her, at least not yet, anyway. I imagined she'd grovel, tell me she was sorry and beg for forgiveness, which incidentally, I would never have given. I thought she'd try to somehow undo the damage. At least try and convince me that she wasn't as bad as I thought, that I'd got it all wrong.

'So that's it; you and Marco decided to destroy my life for twenty-five thousand pounds and the last fourteen years as my best friend was all a lie, is that it?'

She doesn't answer but walks over to the wardrobe, throws open the doors and drags a suitcase out from the back of it. She hurls it onto the bed and unclips it, throwing the lid back.

'I'd have given you the money if you'd asked, Carrie,' I say, quietly.

She spins around from the bed, her eyes blazing. 'And there it is: if I'd asked. I didn't want to ask; I didn't want to have your fucking wealth rammed down my throat yet again. You could never let me forget how rich you are and how poor I am; how lucky I am to have a rich friend like you. Why should I ask? You're only rich because of an accident; you've done nothing to deserve it. Nothing. You're bone fucking lazy and barely scraped a crappy degree, because you couldn't be bothered to do any work. You don't even need a job but one of your rich friends magically happens to know someone who's looking for someone just like you. You didn't even have to try, just turn up and flutter your eyelashes because you got the looks too; talk about unfair.' She walks to the wardrobe, grabs a handful of hangers, drags the clothes out and hurls them into the suitcase. She turns to me.

'Do you know what, Mia? It's actually a relief that it's all out in the open now because I don't know how much longer I could have pretended to be your friend. Why do you think I made sure I went to a different university? To get away from you, Mia, so I could have a life of my own and not have to look out for you and your fucking car crash of a life. The dog-rough boyfriends you always went for, because you thought they were so dangerous and sexy. I could see them for exactly what they were because they came from the same place as me: good-looking losers who couldn't believe that someone like you would even look at them twice, never mind do everything they asked, no matter how degrading.'

She stalks to the wardrobe, wrenches another handful of clothes from the rail and marches back to the suitcase.

'That's why it was so easy. I told Marco to behave like an utter pig and bingo, you were hooked, just as I knew you'd be. He couldn't believe anyone would allow themselves to be treated as badly as you did and come back for more. He thinks you're a complete joke: a pathetic excuse for a woman.'

'It must have hurt, though,' I say, quietly.

'What?'

'Marco. In bed with me. You can't fake that.'

'Don't kid yourself.'

She turns to her case and begins to shove every-thing inside but she wasn't quick enough; I saw the doubt in her eyes.

'Well, for someone faking it,' I say, 'he couldn't get enough of me. Every which way and everywhere.

Every time we met, we ended up having sex and we didn't have to do that, did we? I bet you noticed he was a bit more adventurous in bed after he met me, so at least you got the benefit.'

She doesn't answer and roughly pulls the suitcase closed, forcing it down to get it to shut.

'You could ask him,' I taunt. 'See what he says.'

She won't look at me and I smile.

'Only you won't, will you, Carrie? Because you'll see the lie in his eyes and once you've seen it, you won't be able to unsee it.'

She hauls the case off the bed and stands it upright on the carpet.

'I'll take this with me now and come back for the rest tomorrow.'

'That's up to you.' I saunter over to the bedroom door. 'If you want to risk it. I'll be leaving the bin bags on the pavement outside the front of the apartments tonight. If you're lucky, they might still be there tomorrow.'

'You can't do that.'

'Is that right?'

I continue out of the bedroom and into the kitchen. I hear her following me. I walk over and pick up the kettle, fill it from the tap and put it on to boil.

'Don't you dare leave my stuff outside.' Her voice is low with barely contained anger.

'Or what?' I ask. 'You've already tried to poison me; what else are you going to do?'

She glares at me, realising there's nothing she can do.

I turn around, lean against the countertop and fold my arms.

'Although, to be honest, that's the bit I don't get. Why poison me, Carrie? What were you hoping to achieve?'

She stares at me and smiles.

'Because it was fun, Mia, and it made us laugh.'

25

'I'll ring Marco. Get him to come and help me with my stuff. Either that, or I'll come tomorrow and pick it up if you promise not to throw it out on the street.'

She has a taunting look on her face, as if the thought of Marco coming here will be so terrifying that I'll do anything she asks to prevent that.

'Ring him,' I say, with a smile, pouring boiling water over a teabag. 'It'll be quite novel to talk to a dead man.' The taunting look vanishes, replaced by uncertainty. She wasn't expecting me to say that. 'Your choice,' I pick up the mug of tea and saunter past her, towards the lounge. 'But if those bags aren't gone tonight, they're going out on the street. I might even throw them out of the window. Much quicker than taking them all down in the lift.'

She doesn't reply. I go into the lounge and sit down on the sofa. After a few moments, I hear the sound of her talking quietly. She's ringing him.

So he's coming here.

I'm going to see the man who, for the last nine months, I believed I'd murdered.

And I'm not at all afraid; my mind is clear but more to the point, there's a camera outside the front door which will be filming his, and Carrie's, every move. I realise that I want to see him – no, I *need* to see him, to lay his ghost to rest. To cleanse him from my mind. I drink my tea and imagine what it will be like to see him again. There's silence from the kitchen now, and just as I decide that she's going to hide out there until Marco arrives, she appears in the doorway.

'He's coming.' She glares at me, as if I'm the one who's tricked and poisoned her.

'How lovely,' I say. 'It'll be just like old times.'

'You're mad.' She stares at me with loathing, and I try to understand what it is I've done to make her hate me so much.

'I'm not; even though you tried to make me think I was. It's not my fault you were born poor, Carrie. It's just an accident of birth. I wasn't born rich either. I had to lose both parents to get my money.'

She snorts with disgust. 'Whining again. Poor me. That's so typical of you and your type. Over-privileged and spoilt rotten and thinks the whole world revolves around them. Everything is about money and fucking class and going to the right school or university, isn't it? You have absolutely no idea what life is like for normal people who have to scrape a living while you live in luxury. No idea that the expensive clothes you buy and don't even bother wearing cost more than most people earn in a month.'

'And you know, do you?' I ask. 'Because you went to a private school and live in an expensive area of London, so you're hardly working class, are you? Hardly normal, even though you pretend to be. Always banging on about giving back and the rising cost of living and people wasting money on art and boring people half to death about it. What do you actually do about all this social inequality, Carrie? Nothing, that's what. You're all talk. A champagne socialist.'

She glares at me, her face red, but doesn't answer. Her phone bleeps and she looks at it briefly before turning away and walking down the hallway. I put down my mug and jump up off the sofa and follow her. I watch as she goes into her bedroom, grabs a suitcase and wheels it into the hallway, opens the front door and pushes it outside and stands it next to the lift. She repeats the process until all of her belongings are piled up next to the lift. She stands there, waiting for him. Picking up my front-door key, I come outside and position myself on the landing, making sure I'm in full view of the camera. It can't be long now; he must be getting here soon. Her phone bleeps and she glances down at the screen; he's here, I know he is.

'I hope he's going to come up and help you with all those bags.'

She ignores me, refusing to look up at me. It hits me that she's nervous. 'What's the matter?' I ask. 'Worried that Marco's going to see what he's been missing for all these months and find you wanting?'

Anger flares in her eyes but the sound of the lift bell interrupts us and we both look at the doors as they open. He looks different, is my first thought, when he steps out of the lift. Less, somehow.

When he sees me, he looks shocked. He frowns.

I smile.

It throws him; he wasn't expecting that. He looks

towards Carrie and they share a look before he grabs hold of a suitcase.

'Nothing to say?' I demand, pulling myself up to my full height. 'No words for the woman you deceived and stole from?'

He lets go of the suitcase and strides quickly towards me, stopping inches from my face. I see Carrie hurriedly follow him until she's right behind him.

'You deserved it. Rich bitch. You have so much money, you don't know what to do with it. It was a pleasure taking it off you.' He spits the words at me and I laugh. He can't hide the surprise on his face. He used to talk to me like that all of the time and I'd tell him he was wrong and try to justify myself to him, forgetting that he was only too happy for me to spend my money on him.

'Let's go, Marco,' Carrie says. 'Just leave it. She's not worth bothering with.'

His body moves but his eyes never leave my face.

'Was it worth it, though, Marco? Because twenty-five thousand isn't going to get you very far, not at London prices. Or are you going to be like Robin Hood and give it all away to impoverished children? Do the right thing? Put your money where your socialist mouth is?'

He doesn't answer and Carrie pulls on his arm.

'No. I thought not,' I sneer. 'You're just like her: all talk and no walk. Pathetic.'

He leans forward, his eyes blazing, the Marco I thought I knew back for a moment.

'You made it *so* easy, Mia, so ridiculously easy. "I killed him, Carrie!"' He mimics my accent in a high-pitched voice, like he used to do. 'Too frightened and weak to go and check if the man you'd just shot was actually dead. Too scared to face up to what you'd done, content to let Carrie clear up your mess like she always did. You're a joke, Mia, and every minute I spent with you felt like an hour. A tedious, boring hour.'

His mouth is twisted, his eyes blazing and I can feel the anger emanating off him. Carrie peers at me from behind him, the desperation to leave showing in her eyes.

I reach out my hands and grab him roughly by his collar and yank him towards me. I kiss him full on the lips, grinding my mouth into his, only letting go of him when he manages to wrench himself away.

'You're mad. Insane.' His eyes are round in shock; Carrie stares at me from behind him, surprise on her face. And fear, there's fear there, too.

'Just giving you a reminder of what you're miss-ing.' I laugh, and realise that I'm enjoying myself. 'Because you didn't need to fake that, did you? The sex. Those minutes didn't feel like hours, did they, Marco?'

He turns without another word and storms to the lift doors. Carrie rushes behind him, jabbing the lift button with her finger, eager to leave, to get away from me.

The lift doors open and the pair of them haul the bags and suitcases inside, neither of them looking at me. There's barely enough room for them to get inside with it all and they squeeze in, my last sight of them standing awkwardly at the front as the doors close on them.

I stand immobile for a moment and then turn and walk into the apartment and close the door.

It's over.

Almost.

26

I rather like living on my own; it's been over three weeks since Carrie left and I haven't felt the slightest bit lonely or nervous about being alone. I like being on my own because I can do exactly as I wish without having to consider anyone else. When I cast my mind back and have a good think about it, Carrie wasn't even here that much anyway; she was always working late, or rather, pretending to. And she wasn't much fun either; always so serious and banging on about work and making me too afraid to mention anything to do with money in case I offended her. Ranting on about the environment and politics and other tedious, worthy stuff that bored the arse off everyone.

Marco's welcome to her and her hideous, high-waisted knickers. Now I can do exactly as I like without her judging me or making me feel inferior and shallow.

I'm going to erase all trace of her from my apartment by having a major revamp: all new decor and new furniture. Basically, doing all of the things that I've been wanting to do for a very long time but didn't for fear of upsetting Carrie because of her working-class attitude about how I spend my own money.

The first room to have a makeover will be her old bedroom; it's going to be turned into a dressing room and every wall will have bespoke, fitted wardrobes to fit all of my clothes in. Next will be my room: a brand new, super king size bed, new bedding and some rather sumptuous wallpaper to match. It's all still in the planning stages and I'm in the process of choosing colours and looking at swatches, which is very exciting. And quite time-consuming too. I'm enjoying myself immensely and I want to take my time because it has to be absolutely perfect. I should have done it a long time ago, because it's not as if I can't afford it. Still, better late than never.

Sebastian insists that I'm to stay at his whilst it's all going on and I've said I will but quite honestly, that's not going to happen because we're not going to be together for very much longer. I'll book into a hotel or maybe I'll rent one of those little serviced apartments as the makeover is going to take a few months. Sebastian is very sweet and attentive but he's also a little boring. He was never going to be my forever partner, if I ever have one at all, so it's not as if I've promised him anything. I've never told him that I love him so I haven't deceived him in any way. It's not my fault that he's fallen in love with me. We're still together for now but soon, very soon, it's going to be over.

I just have to think of a nice way of getting rid of him, although realistically, I know that he's going to be devastated. It means leaving my job but I'm okay with that; it's time for a change, or maybe I won't bother working at all. I felt forced into getting a job when I left uni because of Carrie and her ridiculous work ethic. The thought of her disapproving expression made me feel shallow and lazy, that I should occupy myself with gainful employment but now I'm beginning to think, why should I? Imi and Maria have never worked a day in their lives and although Suki is employed by her father, it's only as a tax dodge. She never actually does anything. Most of my other girlfriends don't work either, now I come to think of it. And it's selfish, really, isn't it, taking a job when you don't need it because you're depriving someone else of the opportunity?

Also, now that Carrie's no longer living here, I won't have to suffer her disgusted looks at any men that I might bring home, which is an absolute bonus. No more looking down her nose at my choice of lover or telling me to be careful. As if I'm some sort of halfwit who can't be trusted to look after myself. There were so many times that I didn't bring men home to my own apartment and it was because of her. Just because she wanted to live like a nun, I had to pretend that I didn't believe in casual sex when actually, I do. Plenty of men live their lives having one-night stands, so why shouldn't I? Sex doesn't have to be meaningful, does it? Sometimes, it can just be sex. So, if I want to bring home someone rough and ready, I will. And actually, she never liked anyone, not even Sebastian, who's the perfect gentleman. Although she lied about Sebastian spiking someone's drink in an attempt to put me off him and foolishly, I believed her. I trusted her judgement over my own.

This is all going through my mind as I spoon coffee into a mug in the staff kitchen and I think, yet again, that I don't know why I tolerated her for so long. I assumed that all her seriousness and worthiness about current debates made her somehow better than me, but I've been proven so wrong, it's laughable. She was a worse person than I am because at least I was loyal to her until she crossed me. I finish eating my lunch – a falafel salad because I've gone right off smoothies for obvious reasons – and put her out of my mind. I only allow myself to think about her for short periods of time because I don't want to dwell on the past; what's done is done and I'm not going to lose any sleep over it. Luckily, once someone has crossed me, I can never manage to think of anything good about them again. I'm not in the least sentimental. Only the bad things that they've done stick in my mind, so I don't have to waste time feeling any sadness about what's happened. As for Marco, he rarely crosses my mind and truthfully, a few more months and we'd have been done, anyway. I'm staring at the kettle, willing it to boil, when Tally appears in the kitchen doorway.

'Mia?' she asks, as if there is someone else in the room besides me when it's obviously empty. It suddenly hits me that I won't miss coming here at all because I won't have to put up with her boring me to

death. And her breath smells and she insists on getting so close when she talks. I stifle a sigh; I suppose
I'll have to offer to make her a coffee as she can see
I'm making one for myself. Which means she'll hang
around and start yapping when all I really wanted to
do was to scroll through my phone for new bedroom
furniture. There's a particularly nice upholstered
chair that I had my eye on and now I'll have to leave
it until later. I swallow down my irritation and turn
around and smile.

'Coffee?' I hold up a cup.

'Um. No. You'd better come with me, Mia; there's
someone here to see you.'

'Me?'

She nods, uncharacteristically reticent.

I put down the cup, turn the kettle off and follow
behind her but instead of going into reception, she
stops outside Sebastian's office and knocks on the
door. He calls out, 'Come in' and she pushes open the
door, indicates with a nod of her head for me to go in
and pulls the door closed behind me the minute I'm
inside. Sebastian is sitting behind his desk and a man
and woman are standing in front of his desk. They
turn to look at me as I walk in.

'Miss Enderby?' the man asks.

Sebastian jumps up out of his seat and comes

around the desk to me, throwing a glare at the man as he does so. He puts his arm around me and grips my hand tightly as I look in puzzlement at him and then at the man and woman.

'Mia, this is Sergeant Crossland and Constable Stevens. They're here to talk to you.'

'Me?'

'Yes. I think you'd better sit down.'

Sebastian manoeuvres me to a chair and lowers me into it, elderly-relative style, and then perches on the arm of the chair. Out of the corner of my eye, I see the police officers sit themselves down.

'Miss Enderby, I understand a Miss Carrie Jones used to live with you.' Sergeant Crossland asks, leaning towards me.

'Yes, she did. She moved out a few weeks ago to move in with her boyfriend. Is there something wrong?'

'And when was the last time you saw her?' he asks, ignoring my question.

'The night she moved out. Just over three weeks ago. I've messaged her but she's not responded. I've messaged her quite a few times, actually. We had a bit of a falling out before she left, you see, and I think she's still cross with me, even though I tried to apologise.' I realise I'm volunteering far too much information so I clamp my lips together to stop myself gabbling.

There's an awkward pause and then Sergeant Crossland clears his throat and utters the words I've been expecting from the minute I stepped into the room.

'I see. I'm very sorry to have to inform you, Miss Enderby, that Miss Jones is dead.'

* * *

Sebastian is holding a glass of water to my lips and I take a tiny sip. He has his arm around my shoulders and is holding me upright in the chair. I fight down the urge to push his arm away; I know he's concerned but it's suffocating and annoying and I wish he'd leave me the hell alone.

Besides, I didn't really faint; I was faking it.

It's very useful, fainting, because you can opt out for a little while to get yourself in order: recover yourself, give yourself a bit of breathing space to make sure you present the right image and say the right thing. Fainting wasn't in my plans; even though I'd rehearsed what I was going to do in my head many times, when it came to it, I wanted to laugh. Badly. The faint was a way of preventing that because I couldn't trust myself to speak. I suppose I could have passed it off as being hysterical but whichever way you look at it, laughing when you've just been told your best friend is dead is not a good look.

'Do you feel able to continue now, Miss Enderby?'

I nod. 'It's such a shock. How can she be dead?'

A glance passes between the officers and Sergeant Crossland clears his throat again before continuing.

'I'm sorry to have to tell you that Miss Jones and her boyfriend Marco Henderson were both found dead several days ago. From the evidence we've found so far, it appears to have happened soon after you last saw her.'

I stare at him in shock. 'You mean, all these weeks I've been messaging her, she was dead?'

'It would appear so.'

'But how?' I stare at him, wide-eyed in shock. 'What happened? Has there been some sort of accident?'

He coughs and then clears his throat and I think that maybe he should stop doing that, because it's extremely irritating.

'I have to tell you that they both died of bullet wounds but we're not looking for anyone else in connection with their deaths.'

I stare at him uncomprehendingly.

'Bullet wounds? You mean they were shot? I don't understand.'

'There was a note. Left by Marco Henderson. We're investigating but so far have concluded that it was a murder-suicide and as I said, we're not anticipating looking for anyone else in connection with their deaths. Marco Henderson was in possession of a gun and he shot Miss Jones at point-blank range before turning the gun on himself. Unfortunately, their bodies weren't found for several weeks and it was only when the landlord arrived for a property inspection that they were discovered.'

'Oh my God.' I look up at Sebastian and he tightens his grip on my shoulders. 'How can this be happening, Sebastian? How can Carrie be dead?' I begin to cry and he rubs my back gently.

I hear murmurings from the police officers and the scrape of chairs as they stand up. Sebastian thanks them and I force myself to look at them, wiping the tears from my face.

'Is that it?' I ask. 'She's dead and that's it? He's got away with it? You say there was a note, what did it say?'

'I'm very sorry, Miss Enderby, but as Marco Henderson is dead, we've closed our investigation. The, er, next of kin have possession of the note so you'd have to speak to them about that.'

'Next of kin?'

'Yes. Miss Jones's family have been contacted. I understand her sister is organising the funeral. I'll arrange for someone to give you the details of the solicitor dealing with her estate if you wish to liaise with the family.'

I keep the surprise from my face; Carrie will hate her family having control of her funeral, as she had nothing to do with any of them. I don't think she was lying about that. They'll get any money she had, of course, because she won't have made a will, and that'll be the only thing they care about.

'Thank you.' Not that I'll be going. Or sending flowers. Or contacting the solicitor. If anyone should ask, I'll tell them that it's all too upsetting and I'd rather remember Carrie in my own way.

The police hover around for a moment and then Sebastian ushers them out of the office and several minutes later, he's back.

'How are you, darling?'

'In shock,' I whisper. 'Total shock.'

He pulls me to him and holds me tightly.

'You said that he was controlling, her boyfriend,'

he murmurs as he strokes my back. 'If only she'd listened to you.'

If only she hadn't crossed me.

If only they hadn't underestimated me.

Killed with the gun that they made me believe I'd killed Marco with.

There's something poetic about that, isn't there?

27

The text arrived today. No message, just the details for ten different bank accounts.

I've been expecting it because both funerals are over; Carrie's was last week and Marco's was yesterday. They were both cremated and that means that there is now no evidence left.

Not that the police were looking.

The matter is now closed, I think is the correct way of putting it. I didn't go to either of their funerals, although I knew when and where they both were. I was tempted to attend Carrie's just to get a look at her awful family and hear what they had to say about her, but I managed to talk myself out of it. It would have been a bit risky because I didn't know if I could keep the heartbroken best friend act up for more than ten minutes.

Anyway, I have to send a total of one hundred thousand pounds to the different accounts by close of play today. Very clever, when you think about it, because sending the whole amount to one account would require a trip to the bank to ask them to process it whereas I can do it all online. I might still get a call from the bank, or maybe not, because I have a lot of money with them in various accounts and investments – millions, not hundreds of thousands – and they don't like to question me too much in case they upset me. I'll mix the payments up slightly, make them uneven amounts to make it look as if I'm paying for goods or a service. Which is true, in a way.

So, it's done. Not that I got my hands dirty. No, someone else did the dirty work, someone we'll call the professional, someone who doesn't make mistakes and made sure that Carrie and Marco's deaths could never be traced back to me. Or anyone, actually. There was no need to worry about evidence because there wouldn't have been any; it was a murder-suicide without a shadow of a doubt. The professional who dealt with them was so confident of his capabilities (I assume it was a man) to have Carrie and Marco's deaths declared a murder-suicide that he demands payment only when the deed is done, the police case closed, and there is absolutely no possibility of any of it leading back to my door.

Murder on credit.

There is no risk at all that I won't pay because who would be stupid enough to cross someone like that?

Someone from the dark web.

It's ironic really, when you think about it. Carrie thought she was so clever; I clearly remember her derision at me for being so gullible for believing that someone from the dark web had disposed of Marco's body. But I wasn't gullible at all; the reason I believed her so easily was because the dark web wasn't new to me. I knew what it could be used for. I'd used it myself, many years ago, so I knew it definitely existed and wasn't just a myth.

I knew what Carrie told me was perfectly possible.

The first time I made contact with the dark web was through an ex-boyfriend of mine, Zee Zee. A strange name, I'll grant you, and I never did find out what his real name was. And he was strange, too, no doubt about it: monosyllabic and brooding but absolutely mega-hot. His air of danger was what attracted me to him and when he did talk, it was of death and revenge and teardrop tattoos and dark deeds in unheard of places. When I asked him for a contact to help me get rid of a problem, he never even asked me why, and once he'd given me the number, we never spoke of it again.

I remember sending the text: the feeling of excitement and fear. It almost felt unreal as all contact was via messages and I never met, or had any idea who was on the other end of the phone. As the days went by, I remember thinking that Zee Zee was stringing me along; he was laughing at me, playing a joke on me. Although he wasn't the jolly type and he didn't make jokes so this gave me hope that it was real, and they'd do as I asked.

Because I was desperate.

I understood these things took time to arrange but I was nervous; I'd impressed the importance of swift action being required. It had to happen soon because Gramma had arranged a meeting with the solicitor for the following week and it was imperative that she was never able to attend that meeting.

I was already back at my apartment by this time, staying at Gramma's for one night only, as that was as long as I could bear. Also, I knew I had to be as far away from her as possible when it happened. And then it was done and Gramma was dead. And it worked very well, too. I was far, far, away in the company of lots of other people when she died and there was absolutely no suspicion at all about her death. She had a weak heart and I told them she'd been getting a bit confused and the coroner decided that she'd mistakenly taken too many sleeping pills before she went to bed.

The downside was that I had a breakdown. I'd like to say it was because of the guilt about what I'd done but it wasn't; it was the absolute terror of getting caught. I couldn't actually believe that I'd got away with murder and I was petrified that I'd be arrested. I was just waiting for the knock on the door and for my life to be over. I kept having visions of being locked up for the rest of my days and it overwhelmed me.

In my defence, I was very young, not even twenty-years old, so I think I can be forgiven for my inability to cope. Carrie obviously had no idea what I'd done because I've never told a soul. Like everyone else, she assumed that I was weak, flaky and mentally unstable.

That's where the trouble started; my family

doctor totally overreacted and before I knew it, I'd been sectioned for my own good. That's another drawback with private medicine; there's always a vacancy for you, no waiting around for months on an NHS waiting list to get you a bed somewhere. I soon got over my mini-breakdown but by then, I'd been marked as unstable and it's very difficult to change the medical profession's minds once they've made a diagnosis. If I've learned one thing from the experience, it's to be very careful about letting anyone know anything about you, even if they tell you they're trying to help.

Unlike Carrie and Marco, killing Gramma wasn't about revenge for what she'd done to me, although she'd been vile to me for as long as I could remember. No, it was because she was about to extend her rigid control over me for even longer and I couldn't allow her to do that because she was ruining my life.

My parents left me extremely well provided for but until I reached the age of twenty-one, Gramma had complete control over my finances because all of the money was in trust. I was counting down the days until then; Gramma was domineering and controlling and I couldn't so much as breathe without her knowing about it. She even tried to tell me what to wear; said I looked like a tart when all I was doing was dressing in the same way as any other girl of my age. I was living a carefree life at university where I could behave like a normal nineteen-year-old and thoroughly enjoy myself without her knowing about it. I never wanted to go back home to Gramma where I was expected to behave as if I was living in Victorian England.

But she had spies everywhere.

No matter how careful I thought I'd been, she always found out about the unsuitable boyfriends, the occasional drug use, the classes I'd missed, the trouble that seemed to follow me around. Everything that I didn't want her to know about, she found out.

And she wasn't happy about it at all.

I was summoned home at the end of term, and I had no choice but to go, despite my protests that I'd been invited to France for the summer by one of my friends. She threatened to cut off my allowance if I didn't do as she said.

I can remember that train journey even now; how full of rage I was that although I was an adult, I had to do what she said. I hated her with a passion. Gramma never loved me; I see that clearly now. Her precious son had died and left her with me and she never forgave me for being alive when he was dead. I was the image of my mother, too, which didn't help, as Gramma had hated her for taking her boy away. I sat on that train and sobbed and raged to myself and by the time I arrived at Gramma's house, I'd decided that I'd had enough; I was going to tell her that I was responsible for my own life. I was an adult now and she could no longer control me and I was going to live how I wanted and there was nothing she could do about it. In less than two years' time, I would have full access to my money and I'd never have to see her again. She could make life difficult for me in the meantime of course; under the rules of the trust, she had no choice but to pay my university fees and my living costs, I knew she would question every penny extra that I asked for. But she did that already so it wouldn't make any difference; I didn't care, I would get by somehow. My earlier rage had been replaced by confidence and I felt calm and resolved when I entered Gramma's house.

I wasted no time in telling her of my decision and I remember she was calm and even smiled at me. When I'd finished, she said that I obviously had everything figured out and it was up to me if I wanted to behave like a trollop, but I wouldn't be gaining access to my inheritance at age twenty-one. She'd called me back home to tell me that she was going to have the terms of the trust changed and I wouldn't be able to access any money without her permission until I reached the age of thirty. Or maybe thirty-five; she hadn't quite decided yet. She'd already made an appointment with the solicitor to change it but felt it only right to inform me first. I laughed and told her that she couldn't do that; my parents had set up the trust and she couldn't alter it.

But she could.

There was a clause; if it could be proved that I was too immature to be able to manage the funds myself, the terms could be changed. She had all of the proof: snapshots of me on social media falling out of night clubs, my attendance record at university showing that I'd barely attended 50 per cent of my classes, two cautions for being drunk and disorderly; the list went on and on.

I sat silently as she told me all this and I knew then that I couldn't live under her rules for another eleven years.

I simply couldn't do it.

So she brought about her own death. She wasn't doing it because she cared about me; she didn't give a hoot if I ended up dying in a pool of my own money, she just wanted to punish me for being alive. If she'd left me alone to live my life, she might still be here now and I would have been gone from *her* life, so she'd never have had to look at me again.

So, there it is. She didn't cost as much to get rid of as Carrie and Marco; it was only a fraction as much because she was old and her death was almost expected. And two deaths are harder to explain away than one, of course. I have to admit the professional did a very good job because I had no idea exactly how Carrie and Marco were going to die. The less I knew, the better. The only details I did know were that they weren't still living in Marco's flat; they'd moved on. Where to, I don't know. The professional told me this after I'd furnished him with the address; they weren't there, he said, but finding them wouldn't be a problem. And it clearly wasn't. When I did think about what would happen to them, I assumed it would be an accident or something similar. When the police arrived and told me, it truly was a shock, especially hearing they'd been dead for weeks. I didn't like to dwell for too long on the picture that created in my mind. I suppose I could have not had Carrie and Marco murdered and just hoped that they would go off and live their lives and leave me alone. It's not as if I couldn't afford the twenty-five thousand pounds they stole from me; it was nothing.

But I couldn't leave it, and it wasn't because of the

money; it was the betrayal. It was bad enough that Marco was a liar; I could have forgiven that, because he's a man and it's almost expected. No, it was Carrie; I let her into my life in a way that I've allowed no one else in and despite what she said, I was good to her.

What she did hurt.

Besides, who's to say that they wouldn't have come back for more? Who knows what else they might have been planning for me. I could hardly go to the police and report them for stealing because I'd have to explain the reason I'd given the money to them. Admitting that Carrie and Marco fooled me into believing I'd murdered Marco wouldn't have looked good, would it? The police, would, quite rightly, ask me why I'd covered up a murder in the first place. Carrie and Marco had total disregard for my wellbeing, too, so it wasn't just about the money for them; they were enjoying what they were doing to me. Carrie had been poisoning me for weeks but I have no proof that she'd been doing so it would be my word against hers. I could easily have died or been run over by a bus or something when I was having one of my episodes. Would she have cared at all? No, she wouldn't.

I've learned a hard lesson: to never trust anyone ever again.

Not even Sebastian.

And let's face it; I didn't trust him because I suspected he was poisoning me. Not that it matters now because we're not together any more. After the news of Carrie's death, Sebastian went into full-on care mode and frankly, I couldn't stand it. I felt smothered and extremely irritated and I thought it best to finish with him before he could see how much he annoyed me. He was devastated as I knew he would be; even more so when I told him I wouldn't be working at the gallery any more. I think he had some hope that he might win me back, but I told him firmly that, no, that wasn't going to happen. I said that the news of Carrie's death had affected me deeply but more than that, it had made me realise that although I liked him immensely, I didn't love him and that I couldn't ever see myself feeling that way about him.

I did feel a bit bad, but he's stopped trying to contact me now; he rang constantly for the first week but now he's given up so I assume he's getting over me.

I know he said he loved me but there was always the doubt in my mind that he wouldn't have felt that way about me if I wasn't quite so rich. Sebastian is wealthy but nowhere near as well-off as me and that's not healthy, is it? If I'm going to settle for someone, they have to be at least as rich as I am so I know that they're completely genuine. Besides, I don't need to settle for anyone.

I'm fine on my own.

All in all, I think everything has worked out for the best.

So that's it: it's all over.

Now it's time to get on with my life.

28

I take a picture of a plum-coloured sofa from a new website I've found and save it in my makeover album. It's gorgeous and I think I'll be ordering one once I've made a final decision on the colour scheme. I've amassed a large collection of photographs and samples now and I'll soon have enough to start making some decisions. I look at my watch to see that it's a quarter to three; I should really make those payments now. The text said close of play today so I'd better get on with it and not leave it until the very last minute.

I go over to the desk and take my laptop out of the drawer and rummage around for the card reader, heaving a sigh of relief when I find it languishing underneath some sheets of paper. I'm sure I have another one somewhere in the apartment but now wouldn't be a good time to have to start looking for it. I put it on top of the desk and fire up my laptop. While I wait for it to open, I take a photograph of each set of the bank details I've been sent to make it easier to enter them before going into the bedroom and retrieving my debit card from my purse.

By the time I get back to the lounge, my laptop is ready so I sit down and log into my bank account. I rarely bother to check my account because I have money automatically transferred from my savings when the balance falls below five thousand pounds. I don't like to keep too much in there because my savings accounts pay a decent interest rate.

My current account screen comes up and I'm surprised to see that there's only just over three thousand pounds in there. What's happened to the automatic transfer? Not that it matters on this occasion; I have to transfer a hundred thousand pounds from my savings to pay the professional his payments anyway, so I'll add a bit more on.

Something looks strange about the screen and it takes me a moment to understand what it is; the five savings accounts, ISAs and bonds that I have with this bank all have a balance of one pound. Obviously a glitch but I can't help a small nugget of concern growing in the pit of my stomach. I don't have time for long, boring conversations with bank personnel. I need to make those payments now. Too late, I realise that I should have spent hours searching for furniture *after* I'd made the transfers and not before.

I click on my top saver account that has more than two-hundred and fifty thousand pounds in it and when the screen loads, I stare at it in disbelief.

One pound.

I look at my watch; it's now twenty past three. I try to ignore the rising panic. I open up another tab and log into my savings account with another online bank and wait for it to load. I don't have time to deal with the bank now, it can wait until after I've done the transfers. I'll be having strong words with them, though, because it's really not good enough. Thankfully, this bank doesn't require a card reader, just a code sent directly to my phone. Fingers poised over the keys, I stare open-mouthed in horror as the screen opens.

Total balance: one pound.

I open up another tab and log into my remaining investment accounts.

All have a balance of one pound.

I snatch up my phone and press the keys to ring

the bank and then cancel the call. Getting up from the chair with a mounting sense of dread, I go over to the chest of drawers and pull open the drawer where I keep all of the unopened statements and financial papers that come through the post. Maybe the banks have moved my accounts and written to me and I don't know about it because I never open the letters.

But even as I tell myself this, I know the truth before my eyes confirm it.

The drawer is empty.

My legs give way beneath me and I slump to the floor. My phone is still in my hand and I open up one of my banking apps and press the button to call them. I know that it's futile but I still do it, hoping against hope that I'm wrong. The call is answered and I click through the options until I'm finally speaking to a real-life person.

By the time I end the call, it's confirmed.

Everything is gone.

I open one of the savings accounts on my app and scroll through; there are regular withdrawals of the maximum amount allowed transferred to the same account each and every day until the balance dropped to one pound. The account the money transferred to is not one I recognise but the name on the account is.

C Jones.

The customer service assistant told me that I would have received text alerts about these transfers as they were made and that I must have confirmed the account set up. I checked the mobile phone number with her that the alerts were sent to.

It wasn't my number.

I didn't argue with her because there would be no point. I know who's done it and I know I'll never get it back.

Carrie.

She didn't drug me for fun; she drugged me so she could steal all of my money. She knew I never opened any letters and simply stuffed them into the drawer, she knew I never bothered checking my accounts because I thought it pointless and boring. She knew my philosophy was that I didn't need to concern myself with petty details about finances because when you have a lot of money, it looks after itself and makes even more money for you. I don't need to ring any of my other banks because it's there in front of me on my laptop screen; everything has gone except for a few thousand pounds left in my current account.

Could the money she's stolen be traced, even now? Is there any possibility of getting it back?

I seriously doubt it; Carrie was everything that I'm not: careful, thorough and methodical. She never did anything on impulse. The money will be long gone from the account she transferred it to; she was far too careful to leave it all there. It will have been moved somewhere far away and be completely untraceable. That money will be so well hidden that no one will ever find it.

Not that it matters, because even if it were somehow possible to trace it, it's too late for me. I have to pay the professional today: no excuses, no extra time, no extension of credit.

I don't have the money and I have no way of getting it.

I think of Sebastian and dismiss the idea immediately; even if I could somehow persuade him to help me, there's no way he'd be able to lay his hands on that sort of money in a couple of hours. I have other friends who might possibly be able to help me but there's not enough time. No one is going to hand over a hundred thousand pounds without thinking about it very carefully first.

And I can't pay them back. Ever.

I've run out of luck.

I walk through into the hallway and stare at the front door and wonder how long it will take: when he's going to come for me. Whether I'm going to be made an example of.

This is what happens if you renege on our deal.

I'll be used to show what happens if you don't or can't pay: a warning to others not to even think they can escape punishment. I shudder at the thought of how I might die and then I remember the sleeping tablets in my bedroom. How many would it take to go to sleep and never wake up? Will anyone miss me? Maybe Sebastian will for a short while. A few of my friends perhaps, but not for long. I'll soon be forgotten.

You'll go too far one day Mia, and then what will you do?

Gramma's words. She was right. Today is that day. If I hadn't arranged to have Carrie and Marco killed, I wouldn't be a dead woman walking. I go into the kitchen, take a glass from the cupboard and fill it to the brim with water and then walk slowly to my bedroom.

There is no doubt that I'm going to die. The only choice I have is how.

I close the bedroom door, cross to the window and pull the curtains tightly closed to block out the sunlight.

This is how it ends.

ACKNOWLEDGEMENTS

When I published my first book as an indie author six years ago, I never knew writing would become such a huge part of my life. Being used to *doing it all*, moving from self-publishing to Boldwood Books was a massive step for me but publishing director Isobel Akenhead has smoothed the way brilliantly. I'd like to say a big thank you to her for all of her help and her amazing insight that's already making my writing better. I'd also like to thank the rest of the Boldwood team for their warm welcome, support and help.

A big thank you to my sister and fellow author, CJ Morrow, who has encouraged, helped and guided me from the very beginning. Without her, I would never have written that first book. A huge thank you also, to my husband Peter, for his endless enthusiasm for my writing, for his ideas and for spotting the plot holes where I don't! And, last but not least, thank you to my readers, without whom none of this would be possible.

ABOUT THE AUTHOR

Joanne Ryan lives in the rural county of Wiltshire, South England. She enjoys writing psychological thrillers which explore the dark secrets of seemingly ordinary people. Joanna also writes dark comedy and 'Chick lit' under the pseudonym, Marina Johnson.

Sign up to Joanne Ryan's mailing list for news, competitions and update on future books.

Follow Joanne on social media:

facebook.com/JoanneRyanAuthor

instagram.com/authorjoanneryan

bookbub.com/authors/joanne-ryan

THE

Murder

LIST

**THE MURDER LIST IS A NEWSLETTER
DEDICATED TO SPINE-CHILLING FICTION
AND GRIPPING PAGE-TURNERS!**

**SIGN UP TO MAKE SURE YOU'RE ON OUR
HIT LIST FOR EXCLUSIVE DEALS, AUTHOR
CONTENT, AND COMPETITIONS.**

SIGN UP TO OUR NEWSLETTER

BIT.LY/THEMURDERLISTNEWS

Boldwood

Boldwood Books is an award-winning fiction publishing company seeking out the best stories from around the world.

Find out more at www.boldwoodbooks.com

Join our reader community for brilliant books, competitions and offers!

Follow us
@BoldwoodBooks
@TheBoldBookClub

Sign up to our weekly deals newsletter

https://bit.ly/BoldwoodBNewsletter